THE CAT WHO
HAD 60 WHISKERS

THE CAT WHO HAD 60 WHISKERS

Lilian Jackson Braun

headline

First published in Great Britain in 2007
by HEADLINE PUBLISHING GROUP

1

Cataloguing in Publication Data is available from the British Library

Hardback ISBN 978 0 7553 3854 2

Typeset in Times by Avon DataSet Ltd,
Bidford-on-Avon, Warwickshire, B50 4JH

Printed and bound in Great Britain by
Clays Ltd, St Ives plc

Headline's policy is to use papers that are natural, renewable and
recyclable products and made from wood grown in sustainable
forests. The logging and manufacturing processes are expected to
conform to the environmental regulations of the country of origin.

HEADLINE PUBLISHING GROUP
A division of Hachette Livre UK Ltd
338 Euston Road
London NW1 3BH

www.headline.co.uk
www.hodderheadline.com

Dedicated to Earl Bettinger,

The Husband Who . . .

ACKNOWLEDGMENTS

To Earl, my other half – for his husbandly love, encouragement, and help in a hundred ways.

To my research assistant, Shirley Bradley – for her expertise and enthusiasm.

To Becky Faircloth, my office assistant – who's always there when I need her.

To my editor, Natalee Rosenstein – for her faith in *The Cat Who* from the very beginning.

To my literary agent, Blanche C. Gregory, Inc. – for a lifetime of agreeable partnership.

To the real-life Kokos and Yum Yums – for their fifty years of inspiration.

PROLOGUE

Overheard at an alfresco party in Moose County, 400 miles north of everywhere:

WOMAN IN BLUE SHETLAND SWEATER: 'I have never heard of such a thing! And I've been a veterinarian for twenty years!'

MAN WITH LARGE MOUSTACHE: 'What can I say? I counted them myself.'

WOMAN: 'You might have miscounted.'

MAN: 'Would you like to count them yourself? If I'm right, you can report the evidence to a scientific journal. If I'm wrong, I'll take you to dinner at the Mackintosh Inn.'

WOMAN: 'Fair enough! We'll do it the next time you bring him in for a dental prophylaxis.'

One

The man with the large moustache (a well-groomed pepper and salt) was Jim Qwilleran, columnist for the *Moose County Something* and transplant from Down Below, as locals called the metropolitan areas to the south. They themselves, for the most part, were descended from the early settlers, and they had inherited the pioneer fortitude, sense of humor, and appreciation of individuality.

They enjoyed the Qwill Pen column that ran twice weekly . . . accepted the fact that he lived alone in a converted apple barn, with two cats . . . and admired his magnificent moustache.

James Mackintosh Qwilleran had entertained several ambitions in his youth Down Below: first to play second base with the Chicago Cubs, then to act on the Broadway stage, and later to write for the *New York Times*. He had certainly never wanted to be the richest individual in the northeast central United States! How it happened was a tale 'stranger than fiction'.

'Aunt Fanny' Klingenschoen probably knew what she was doing when she made him her sole heir.

Qwilleran established a philanthropic organization: the Klingenschoen Foundation, which went to work improving the quality of life in Moose County. Medical, scholastic, cultural, and infrastructural improvements were made possible by the K Fund, as it was known to one and all.

To everyone's surprise, other old-moneyed families were inspired to put their fortunes to work for the public good. A music center, two museums – one in a mansion – and a senior recreation facility were in the works.

Everything's going too smoothly, Qwilleran thought, with the pessimism of a seasoned newsman. 'What's your fix on the situation, Arch?' he asked his old friend from Chicago.

Arch Riker was now editor in chief of the *Something*. He shook his head morosely. 'When there's so much money floating around, somebody's gonna get greedy.'

4

(Visitors from far and wide – in formal attire – had paid five hundred dollars a ticket for a preview of the mansion, called the Old Manse.)

It was a late evening in August. Qwilleran and the cats had been enjoying a cozy evening in the barn. He had read to them from the *Wall Street Journal*, and they all had a little ice cream.

The barn was an octagonal structure of fieldstone and weathered shingles more than a century old. Indoors, all the old wood surfaces and overhead rafters had been bleached to a honey color, and odd-shaped windows had been cut in the walls.

Where once there had been lofts for storing apples, now there was a ramp winding around the interior, with balconies at three levels.

Later in the evening, the Siamese deserted the reading area and chased each other up and down the ramp, then dropped like flying squirrels onto the sofa on the main floor. The living areas were open plan, surrounding a huge fireplace cube, its stacks rising to the roof forty feet overhead.

It was almost eleven P.M., and Koko and Yum Yum were being unduly attentive; it was time for their bedtime snack.

Proceeding in slow motion, to tantalize the anxious cats,

he rattled the canisters of Kabibbles and dusted off their two plates with exaggerated care. They watched hungrily. Koko appeared to be breathing heavily.

Suddenly Koko switched his attention to the wall phone that hung between the kitchen window and the back door. He stared at it for a minute, twitching his ears nervously.

Qwilleran got the message. By some catly intuition, Koko knew the phone was going to ring. After a few seconds it rang. How did that smart cat know? Guessing that it would be Polly Duncan, the chief woman in his life, Qwilleran answered in a facetiously syrupy voice: 'Good evening!'

'Well! You sound in a good mood,' she said in the gentle voice he knew so well. 'What are you doing?'

'Nothing much. What are you doing?'

'Shortening my new dress a couple of inches.'

'Whoo-ee!'

Ignoring the comic wolf whistle, she went on, 'It's much too long, and I thought I'd wear it with some Scottish accessories Sunday afternoon, since the party's celebrating Dr Connie's return from Scotland. Would you consider wearing your Highland attire, Qwill?'

Although he had once rebelled at wearing what he called a 'skirt', he now felt proud in a Mackintosh kilt with a dagger in his knee sock. After all, his mother had been a Mackintosh.

'What was Connie doing in Scotland? Do you know?'

'She earned her degree from the veterinary school in Glasgow twenty years ago, and she goes back to visit friends. Did you know her cat has been boarding with Wetherby?'

'No! How does he get along with Jet Stream?'

'Connie introduced them when Bonnie Lassie was a kitten, and now Jet Stream acts like her big brother. And,' she went on, 'Connie brought Joe a lovely Shetland sweater as a thank-you for boarding Bonnie Lassie.

'Do you realize, Qwill, that the Shetland archipelago, where the wool comes from, has a hundred islands! . . . A hundred islands!' she repeated when he failed to respond.

'It boggles the mind,' he said absently, watching the Siamese trying to get into the Kabibbles canister.

'Well, anyway, I thought you'd like to hear the latest. *À bientôt*, dear.'

'*À bientôt*.'

After the Siamese had finished their bedtime repast and their washing up, Qwilleran escorted them up the ramp to their quarters on the top balcony. They looked around as if they had never seen it before, then hopped into their respective baskets and turned around three times before settling down.

Cats. Who can understand them? Qwilleran thought, as he quietly closed their door.

Returning to his desk at ground level, he wrote about it in his private journal. He was a compulsive writer! When not turning out a thousand words for the Qwill Pen column, he was writing a biography or history of interest in Moose County. And he always filled a couple of pages in his private journal. On this occasion, he wrote:

I've said it before, and I'll say it again: Koko is a remarkable cat! Is it because his real name is Kao K'o-Kung, so he knows he's descended from the royal Siamese?

Or is it because – as I insist – he has sixty whiskers?

He knows several seconds in advance when the phone is going to ring – and also whether the caller is a friend or a telemarketer selling life insurance or dog food.

When crazies bombed the city hall window boxes, Koko knew ten minutes in advance that something dire was going to happen. Why didn't someone read his signals? The police chief was sitting here having a nightcap, and neither of us got the message!

Oh, well! We can't all be as smart as a psychic Siamese!

Two

Qwilleran was a well-known figure in downtown Pickax: tall, well built, middle-aged, always wearing an orange baseball cap. He responded to casual greetings with a friendly salute and took time to listen if someone had something to say. There was a brooding look of concern in his eyes that made townsfolk wonder. Some wondered if there had been a great tragedy in his life. His best friends wondered, too, but they had the good taste not to pry. Once he had been seen to help an old lady cross Main Street. When observers commended him for his gallantry, he said, 'No big deal! She just wanted to get to the other side.'

At Lois's Luncheonette, where Qwilleran went for coffee and apple pie and the latest scuttlebutt, customers would say, 'How's Koko, Mr Q?' Humorous mentions about Koko and Yum Yum in the Qwill Pen were awaited by eager readers.

Moose County was said to have more cats per capita than any other county in the state. In Lockmaster County, horses and dogs were the pets of choice.

In cold weather, when the converted barn was hard to heat, Qwilleran moved his household to Indian Village, an upscale residential complex on the north edge of Pickax. There, four-plex apartments and clusters of condos had features that appealed to career-minded singles and a few couples. There was a clubhouse with a swimming pool, meeting rooms, and a bar. There were walking paths for bird-watching along the banks of a creek. And indoor cats were permitted.

The cluster called the Willows had four rather notable occupants: the manager of the Pirate's Chest bookstore, a doctor of veterinary medicine, the WPKX meteorologist, and – at certain times of the year – a columnist for the *Moose County Something*.

Also in residence were six indoor felines: Polly Duncan's Brutus and Catta; Dr Connie Cosgrove's kitten, Bonnie Lassie; Wetherby Goode's Jet Stream; and Jim

Qwilleran's Siamese, Koko and Yum Yum, well known to newspaper readers.

Wetherby Goode (real name Joe Bunker) had a yen for party-giving and a talent for entertaining at the piano. He played 'Flight of the Bumblebee' and 'The Golliwog's Cakewalk' without urging at pizza parties on Sunday afternoons.

Dr Connie's return from Scotland was a good excuse for assembling the residents of the Willows.

The guest of honor was wearing a Shetland sweater in a luscious shade of blue. The host was wearing the taupe sweater she had brought him from Scotland, and there were Shetland scarfs for Polly and Qwilleran.

'Connie, may I ask why you chose to get your degree in Scotland?' Qwilleran asked.

She said, 'The vet school at University of Glasgow is internationally known – and has been for many years. It's noted for teaching excellence and research. Early studies of animal diseases later resulted in advances in human medicine.'

Wetherby sat down at the piano and played a medley of songs from *Brigadoon* with the flourishes that were his trademark.

Qwilleran recited Robert Burns's poem 'A Man's a Man for All That'. Toasts were drunk. And then the pizza was delivered.

During the meal there was plenty of talk: mostly about Hixie Rice, who was promotion director for the newspaper and a resident of Indian Village. She was masterminding the new senior center on a pro bono basis . . . She had worked so hard on the Fourth of July parade, and then it was rained out by the hurricane . . . and then vandals had trashed the front of the city hall after she had done wonders in beautifying it. As for romance, she had been unlucky.

Qwilleran, who had known Hixie Down Below and had been instrumental in her coming to Moose County, had little to say.

She was unlucky, that was all. She was talented, spirited, and a tireless worker – but unlucky. There was a Hixie jinx that followed her, and now she was charged with the responsibility for the new senior center.

The *Something* had announced a contest to name it, with an entry blank printed on the front page.

Joe Bunker said, 'That was very clever of the *Something*. To make three entries, you have to buy three papers.'

Qwilleran said, 'You weathermen are too smart, Joe. We thought no one would notice our scheme.'

Polly said, 'The official ballot box has been in the bookstore, and it created a lot of traffic. Judd Amhurst kept moving it around so the carpet wouldn't wear out in one spot. Judd retired early from his job with Moose County Power, and he still had plenty of pep. He's manager of the Lit Club and he volunteers at the animal shelter, where he washes dogs.'

'What's next on the program at the Lit Club?' Qwilleran asked.

'There's a retired professor in Lockmaster who's an authority on Proust, and he's coming to lecture . . . It would be nice, Qwill,' Polly said, 'if you'd put him up at the barn for one overnight.'

Qwilleran said, 'I'm sure it would make a good perk in addition to the modest stipend you can afford. Koko has been making aerial attacks. On ailurophobes. I hope this speaker likes cats.'

The foursome moved to the deck for coffee and Polly's homemade chocolate brownies. Jet Stream accompanied them on a leash, because of the recent scare about rabid wildlife. There had been a time when cats were free to visit the creek and watch the fish and birds. Now there was evidence of rabid skunks, raccoons, and foxes. What had happened?

Joe explained, 'Too many house pets are getting mixed up with rabid wildlife!'

Polly said she had never understood the nature of rabies.

'An infectious disease common to some forms of

wildlife,' Dr Connie said. 'It's transmitted through the saliva when rabid animals get into fights with household pets and bite them. The best safeguard is the leash or the cage. Otherwise they'll see something move on the bank of the creek and be off for some fun!'

Qwilleran said, 'We never had rabid animals in downtown Chicago – only kids with slingshots and careless truck drivers.'

Then Qwilleran broached the subject of Koko's sixty whiskers, and Dr Connie said, 'I can't imagine that Koko was enthusiastic about your counting them.'

Qwilleran said, 'I gave him a mild sedative that is used in the theater when cats are to be onstage.' He was the first to say he had to go home and feed the cats. The women said the same thing. As a farewell, Joe sat down at the piano and played 'Kitten on the Keys' very fast!

Someone said, 'We must do this again soon,' and everyone agreed.

Qwilleran escorted Polly to Unit One and went in to say good night to Brutus and Catta, as he always did.

After Joe's fast pace at the piano and after the nonstop friendly chatter, Qwilleran welcomed a quiet evening with the Siamese.

Driving home, Qwilleran remembered growing up in Chicago and hearing his mother play 'Kitten on the Keys'

14

– and marveling at how her fingers flew over the keyboard. Now Joe Bunker played it twice as fast! Where did he get his nervous energy? He grew up in the town of Horseradish, inhaling all those powerful fumes. Joe had a cousin with a PhD in corvidology, and she was as wacky as he was.

Entering the barnyard, he saw Koko cavorting in the kitchen window. He knew what that meant.

Two cats – Where's our dinner? We're starving!

One cat – There's a message on the phone.

The call was from Judd Amhurst, one of the three judges assigned to select a new name for the facility.

'Qwill! We've got the name! And it's perfect! It'll be in tomorrow's paper, but if you can't wait, give me a call.'

Judd lived at the Winston Park apartment complex – just across from the bookstore where the judging was scheduled to take place.

Never comfortable with unanswered questions, Qwilleran phoned him immediately. 'Judd, don't keep me in suspense!'

'Well, Maggie, Thornton, and I met in one of the community rooms at the bookstore. Big table! Bushels of entries! We started reading them aloud. Most were ordinary. Some were silly. A few had possibilities. Then

Thornton read one from Bill Turmeric of Sawdust City—'

'I know him!' Qwilleran interrupted. 'He writes clever letters to the editor.'

'You'll like this one! It's complete with a motto!' Then he read: 'Senior Health Club – Good for the Body, Good for the Mind, Good for the Spirit.'

'Sign me up!' Qwilleran said. 'Am I old enough?'

'I thought you'd like it, Qwill. We sorted through all of them, but this was the best.'

'What's the prize?'

'The paper's giving two hundred dollars, and there are gift certificates from merchants.'

'Well, thanks for tipping me off. I'll devote Tuesday's column to the Old Hulk – Its Past and Future.'

Qwilleran started making notes for his Tuesday column:

- Feed-and-seed warehouse.
- Served farmers for more than a century.
- Called the Old Hulk.
- Typical warehouse: flat roof, no windows, loading dock.
- Interior: nothing but open space with lofts for sacks of feed and seed, connected by ramps. In-town location no longer serviceable to today's farmers,

who prefer more accessible outlets located at handy
locations around the county.

- Property vacant for several years.
- Will need public entrances, windows, five floors connected by stairs and elevators, plumbing, electricity,
  and a lot of paint and carpet and ideas!
- Why not a roof garden?

In his journal he would write:

The Old Hulk was a piece of abandoned property on
the north edge of Pickax, recently purchased by the
Scottish community and given to the city as a senior
center, along with a grant covering complete
remodeling, redecorating, and furnishing.

In the nineteenth century, Scottish shipbuilders had
come to Moose County to build three-masted
schooners using the two-hundred-foot pine trees for
masts. When steam replaced sail, they turned to
house building and did well, as attested by their man-
sions in Purple Point and their support of community
projects. The senior center was to be their thank-you.

As for the property chosen, it had been a feed-and-
seed depot and warehouse where farm wagons came
to stock up. New modes of transportation had

replaced it with several small depots around the county. The Old Hulk, as it was called, became a hangout for kids, feral cats, and who knows what else. Now, architects and builders were donating their expertise and the *Something* was offering the coordinating services of Hixie Rice to the project pro bono.

Later that day, Qwilleran had a phone call from Hixie Rice.

'Guess what? The dog table is back!'

Early in the year an heirloom auction had been staged to raise money for furnishing the new Senior Health Club. Old families donated prized possessions – everything from porcelain teacups to rare items of furniture.

One such was a six-foot library table of ponderous oak construction with bulbous legs at one end; the other end was supported by a life-size carving of a basset hound. It was donated by the office manager of the *Something*, inherited from her wealthy father.

Everyone said: 'It weighs a ton! Bet she's glad to get rid of it. Can she take it as a tax deduction? What's it worth?'

At the auction an unidentified agent made a sealed bid and won the table for . . . ten thousand dollars! It left town on a truck for parts unknown.

Now the dog table was back! . . . donated to the Senior Health Club by an unidentified well-wisher.

Qwilleran asked, 'How will it be used?'

'In the foyer, which is quite large. It'll be a focal point, with magazines on top, and a table lamp . . . Maybe we should have a cat lamp! An artist could do a sculpture of a cat sitting on his haunches and holding the socket in his paws! Do you think Koko would pose? Everybody would come to see our dog table and cat lamp!'

'Hang up!' Qwilleran said. 'You're hallucinating!'

Three

Qwilleran was half an hour late in serving breakfast to the cats on Monday morning. They attacked their plates as if they had been deprived of food for a week. At one point, though, Koko raised his head abruptly and stared at a spot on the kitchen wall. In a few seconds the phone rang, and he returned to the business at hand.

The caller was Lisa Compton, retired academic and wife of the school superintendent. She was also the chief volunteer at Edd Smith's Place, where preowned books were sold for charitable causes.

'Qwill, a chauffeur from Purple Point just brought

in a box of books that made me think of you.'

'The statement raises questions,' he said.

'You'll love them! They're all pocket-size hardcovers – the kind they had before paperbacks. Convenient for reading to the cats – and really quite attractive. Some have decorative covers and gold-printed titles on the spines.'

'What kind of titles?'

'All classics. *Kidnapped, Lorna Doone, Uncle Tom's Cabin* . . . and authors like Guy de Maupassant, Henry James, and Mark Twain.'

Qwilleran said, 'Don't let them get away from you! I'll be right there!'

'May I make a suggestion? Since the box is rather large, you should park in the north lot and come to the back door. It leads right downstairs into Edd Smith's Place.'

Qwilleran liked Lisa. She always thought everything through – not only selling him the books but figuring the easiest way of getting them to his car.

'And by the way, Qwill, there's some Lit Club business to discuss. If you have time.' She used a formal voice that indicated the other volunteers were listening. 'Do you have a few minutes?'

Always interested in a little intrigue, he said, 'See you in ten minutes.'

* * *

Later, in the private meeting room, Lisa said in a low voice, 'This is not for publication, but I'm giving up volunteer work and taking a paid job as manager of the Senior Health Club.'

'Well!' he said in astonishment. 'I'm shocked – and pleased! What does Lyle think about it?'

'He thinks the club is very lucky to get me.'

'I agree!'

'It's a big job of coordination: scheduling activities, handling memberships, finding instructors, finding new ideas—'

'Lisa, you're the only one who can do it. Let me know if there's anything that I can do to help.'

Famous last words, he thought on the way back to the barn. What am I getting into?

Qwilleran collected Famous Last Words and had his readers contributing them too. Someday, he told them, the K Fund might publish a collection. There were examples like:

'You don't need to take an umbrella . . . It's not going to rain.'

'The Road Commission says the old wooden bridge . . . is perfectly safe!'

'Let's not stop to buy gas . . . We're only driving over the mountain.'

And for every gem that was printed, he gave the proud contributor a fat yellow lead pencil stamped *Qwill Pen* in gold – trophies that were treasured.

To Arch Riker it was just a lazy columnist's way of letting his readers do all the work. The editor's huff was all an act, of course, Qwilleran told himself with a complacent shrug as the sacks of his fan mail filled the mailroom.

When Qwilleran brought the boxful of books into the barn, Koko came running; Yum Yum came in a sedate second.

Qwilleran placed the treasure trove on the bar, and Koko proceeded to go wild with excitement, a performance leading one to wonder where the books had been. When they were unloaded, however, it became evident that it was the box – not the books – that aroused the cat's interest. *Interest* was a mild word; Koko went berserk over the empty box, inside and out!

Qwilleran called the ESP. 'Lisa! Is it polite to ask who donated these books?'

'Is it polite to ask why you want to know?' she asked teasingly.

'Koko wants to know. It's not the books that interest him so much as the box they came in.'

'It's large,' Lisa said. 'Maybe he wants to set up housekeeping in it.'

'It's not only large – but plain. Just a brown carton without any pictures of Ivory Snow or Campbell's Soup.'

'That's funnier than you think, Qwill. The books came from one of the Campbell families in Purple Point.'

'I wonder where they acquired them. Do you know that family well enough to ask? Tell them Cool Koko wants to know its provenance.'

'They'll love it! They're all fans of the Qwill Pen.'

With shelf space found for the books and a session of reading from *The Portrait of a Lady*, Koko calmed down. The box itself was in the shed along with rubbish and a few garden tools. A do-not-discard note was taped to it; its provenance remained a mystery.

As for Koko, he behaved like a normal house cat for the rest of the day until four o'clock.

Late Monday afternoon, Qwilleran was lounging in his big chair when Koko suddenly appeared from nowhere and jumped to the arm of the chair. His lithe body was taut and his ears pointed toward the kitchen window.

Someone's coming! Qwilleran thought. The cat jumped down and ran to the kitchen, where he could look out the window from the countertop. Qwilleran followed him.

Outside the window was the barnyard – and then a patch of dense woods and a dirt road leading to Main Street and several important buildings. Surrounding a traffic circle were two churches, the public library, a theater arts building, and the grand old courthouse.

Qwilleran waited to see a vehicle coming through the woods. Nothing arrived, but Koko kept on watching. Qwilleran went back to his lounge chair.

At that moment the kitchen phone rang. It was the attorney.

'Qwill! This is Bart! I know this is short notice. Do you have a few minutes? I'm phoning from the courthouse.'

Qwilleran was stunned into silence. Koko had known a call was coming from a building half a mile away!

'Qwill, did you hear me? I said—'

'I heard you, Bart. Koko was diverting my attention, that's all. Come on over.'

'Tell Koko I have a treat for him.'

'Your Uncle George is coming,' he told the cats.

Shortly, the attorney arrived and was joyously greeted by all.

The four of them proceeded single file to the conference table – Qwilleran carrying the coffee, Bart carrying his briefcase, and the cats carrying their tails straight up.

Opening his briefcase, Bart said, 'My wife sent a treat for the cats – something she makes for our brats. They like the sound effects when they crunch it.' He drew a plastic zipper bag from among the documents.

'It's like Italian biscotti but with seasoning of particular interest to cats – my wife says! She calls it biscatti.'

Koko and Yum Yum were allowed to sniff the plastic bag, but it was too early 'for their treat'.

Qwilleran said, 'While you're here, Bart, perhaps you could give me some information about the Ledfield house that's being opened as a museum. Not everyone knows it's called the Old Manse – and has been for the last hundred years. I'm wondering if Nathan Ledfield's grandfather had read Hawthorne's *Mosses from an Old Manse* and incorporated any ideas from his reading. If so, it's a suggestion for the Qwill Pen.'

'Would you like a tour of the house?' Bart asked. 'It can be arranged.'

Then he launched into an explanation of necessary changes in converting a private mansion to a county-owned museum.

'Nathan Ledfield had long employed two assistants:

Daisy Babcock, who handled financial matters, and Alma Lee James, in charge of his collection of art and antiques . . . You may know her parents' art gallery in Lockmaster, Qwill. Alma Lee is very knowledgeable, and her connection with the gallery resulted in some very favorable purchases for the Ledfield collection . . . Is there more coffee?'

As Qwilleran poured, he said, 'Leaving the mansion to the county must have entailed some drastic changes.'

'Not too drastic,' the attorney assured him. 'Alma Lee has been named director of the museum. That involves training museum guides as well as supervising maintenance of the building. Daisy Babcock will act as her assistant, since the finances will be handled by an investment counselor appointed by the county.'

'Then I should see Miss James for a tour of the Old Manse,' Qwilleran assumed.

'Yes, either she or Miss Babcock can show you around . . . If you'll pardon a little in-house gossip: Daisy Babcock resents being demoted to second-in-command. When Nathan Ledfield was boss, Daisy was his fair-haired girl! I wouldn't be surprised if she quits. She's married to one of the Linguini sons but uses her maiden name.'

'Wise choice,' Qwilleran murmured, reflecting that 'Daisy Linguini' would be a fetching name for a trapeze performer but not so good for a financial secretary to a billionaire.

Qwilleran asked, 'Are those the Linguinis who had the wonderful Italian restaurant?' It was a mom-and-pop operation. If a customer was having a birthday, Papa Linguini would come out of the kitchen in his chef's hat, get down on one knee, fling his arms wide, and sing Happy B-ir-r-rthday in an operatic voice. 'Apparently they retired.'

'Yes, and their sons preferred to open a party store and plant a vineyard. They also want to open a winery, but the neighbors along the shore are objecting.'

Before he left, Bart said, 'About visiting the Old Manse: either of the women could show you around and answer your questions, but it might be politic to work with Alma James. Let me break the ice for you. I know she's been dying to see your barn—'

'Half the Western world has been wanting to see my barn. That's okay. How do we go about it?'

'I could drive her over someday, then ease her out if she wants to stay too long.'

'Does she like cats?' Qwilleran asked. 'Koko has been known to react to ailurophobes in peculiar ways.'

'She's from Lockmaster and is more accustomed to dogs and horses.'

'I could put Koko and Yum Yum out in the gazebo.'

'No! No!' said Bart, a confirmed ailurophile. 'It's their barn! Let her adjust. If she begins to itch or sneeze, she won't want to stay so long.'

Qwilleran, detecting a lack of enthusiasm on the attorney's part, asked, 'How do you size up the two women in charge of the Manse?'

'Daisy is always relaxed and friendly. Alma – I never liked that name – is warm or cold, agreeable or reserved, depending on her mood . . . You'll have to excuse me; I grew up with an aunt called Alma, and she let her sons break my toys and squirt me with water pistols.'

That was what Qwilleran liked about Bart – he was human and *honest*.

On his way out, the attorney said, 'I almost forgot. My daughter asks a favor. She's making a survey and would like you to write two words on an index card.' He drew a card and a pen from his pocket. 'You write *cat* on one side of the card and *dog* on the other . . . Sign your initials.'

Qwilleran wrote *dog* on the first side in proper penmanship. On the reverse side he dashed off *cat* in a flamboyant script, crossing the t with a bar an inch long.

'I thank you. My daughter thanks you. She's quite serious about this study – her own idea – although it will never be published.'

'How old is she?' Qwilleran asked.

'Nine going on fifteen. Next summer she wants to extend the survey to Lockmaster,' he said, raising parental eyebrows.

Qwilleran found his copy of *Mosses from an Old Manse* and scanned it for references that might be linked with the mansion in Purple Point.

That night Qwilleran wrote in his journal:

Monday – I thought I had Koko all figured out. He knows when the phone is going to ring!

But today he knew Uncle George was coming from the county building *before the guy had announced his intentions*. What about the biscatti in the briefcase? Did Koko know about that, too?

I sound crazy, and sometimes I feel I'm slipping over the edge.

What I mean is: it's pretty well established that Koko (a) knows what's going to happen. Does he also (b) *make things happen*?

I won't go that far, but I admit he puts ideas in my head. That's nothing new; Christopher Smart knew that a few centuries ago.

But why does Yum Yum's buddy have more on the

ball than most felines? I still say it's because he has sixty whiskers! Regardless of what Dr Connie says and what the scientific literature says, I still maintain my opinion.

How far am I prepared to go?

Perhaps I'd better pipe down? They'll start counting my own whiskers. That would be a joke! Koko transmits, and I receive!

Qwilleran mused whimsically. What an investigative team we'd make! . . . Koko's whiskers transmitting inside information – and my moustache receiving the data.

Four

Qwilleran ended his Tuesday column with a few 'Famous Last Words' submitted by readers. These folk gems of humor arrived in the mailroom of the *Something* – on government postcards. Reader participation was a healthy sign for a small-town paper, and the 'Famous Last Words' obviously came from all walks of life. Almost all were printable, and the best would be published in book form, it was promised, with proceeds going to some worthy cause. The latest were:

'My new kitten is adorable . . . and they assure me he's housebroken.'

'I haven't had a drink for five years . . . so it won't hurt
   to have a little nip.'

'My dog likes to play rough . . . and he never bites!'

'I'm sorry, Officer . . . I thought I had the green light.'

When Qwilleran delivered his Tuesday copy to the office
of the *Something*, he walked down the long hall of the
building and could hear the editor in chief shouting behind
closed doors. It was the kind of angry shouting that is
usually accompanied by waving arms. There was no clue
as to which staff member was getting a roasting.

Qwilleran stopped in the food editor's office. 'What did
you give your husband for breakfast, Mildred?'

'Tell you later! I'm on deadline!' She waved him away.

'What happened?' Qwilleran asked one of the reporters.

'Clarissa Moore went home to Indiana to attend a
funeral, and this morning she sent a wire: she's not coming
back! Arch is wild, and I don't blame him,' the reporter
said. 'For a J student right out of college, she got a lot of
breaks here.'

Qwilleran had done his part to encourage the novice,
and although she was a *good* feature writer, she was hardly
good enough to be forgiven for such cavalier behavior.

Qwilleran asked, 'Does anyone know if she took her
cat? If she took Jerome, she knew she was going for good;

otherwise, she would have left him in her apartment with her neighbors.' He made a mental note to ask Judd Amhurst at the Winston Park apartments.

He disliked unanswered questions.

Deadline for the Tuesday Qwill Pen was twelve noon, and Qwilleran filed his copy with the managing editor according to custom – not late, but not too early either.

Junior Goodwinter glanced at the transcript and rang for the copy boy, and said, 'Do you know a feature writer we could hire? Jill Handley won't be back from maternity leave for a few months.'

'How about running a series of guest features? Make it sound like an honor instead of an emergency, and they'll be vying for the privilege. For their cooperation you can make a contribution to their favorite charity. It would be invitational, of course. I can think of a dozen names without even trying. Bill Turmeric, Dr Abernathy, Mavis Adams, Dr Connie Cosgrove, Wetherby Goode, Thornton Haggis, Judd Amhurst, Polly Duncan—'

'Stop! I think it might work!'

'Whannell MacWhannell,' Qwilleran went on. 'His wife, the astrologer. Silas Dingwall. Maggie Sprenkle can write about the animal welfare program . . .'

'How about setting it up for us?' Junior asked.

Qwilleran said, 'I'm a columnist, I don't do setup.'

* * *

Qwilleran went home to give the cats their noontime treat and consider his own problem: how to write a column on the Old Manse for Friday's Qwill Pen.

His pet theory about the Manse and the Hawthorne book remained to be tested, and the sooner the better. The attorney had been frank about the mansion's personnel, but it wouldn't hurt to get a second opinion.

Maggie and her late husband had owned the estate adjoining the Ledfields'. They had dined together frequently, and Maggie could probably give him some tips.

Qwilleran phoned Maggie and was offered: a nice cup of tea! He said he would come up right away. (Someday the Qwill Pen would address the question of tea – and the difference between an ordinary cup of tea and a nice one.)

He biked to the rear of the Sprenkle Building and was admitted to the small elevator lobby, just large enough for his British Silverlight.

The upstairs apartment – over the insurance and real estate offices – was of Victorian splendor. The five front windows were occupied by Maggie's five 'ladies' from the animal shelter. Tea was ready to be poured.

After the niceties, Qwilleran broached his idea for the Old Manse column. She thought it was splendid.

He stated his case, and the practical octogenarian said, 'I never heard Nathan claim a connection between his grandfather and the author . . . but he never *disclaimed* one either!'

'Mr Barter advised me to arrange an appointment with Miss James or Miss Babcock.'

She paused significantly. 'I think . . . you would find Daisy Babcock . . . amenable to your idea. She's a lovely girl. Alma Lee is a little . . . *starchy*, although I must admit she's an encyclopedia of information on Georgian silver and eighteenth-century crystal. She's not there every day, so you have to make an appointment. She spends three days a week in Lockmaster, where her parents have a gallery of art and antiques.'

She said more, but Qwilleran had made up his mind to choose Daisy. He said, 'The Ledfields have been very generous to the community.'

'Nathan was always a good and generous soul. There was a couple that worked for him – Mr and Mrs Simms, and they were killed in an auto accident, leaving a seven-year-old daughter. Nathan found a good home for her with a family at the church. But he also kept in touch with her, checking her report card at every marking and giving her gifts for birthdays and Christmas – nothing inappropriately expensive but useful and thoughtful. After high school he put her through business school and then hired her to handle his correspondence and personal expenses.'

'Where is she now?' Qwilleran asked.

'His will stipulated that Libby Simms should continue to handle his private matters. He made sure that his lawyers knew her position in the family.'

'A touching story,' Qwilleran murmured. 'How old is she now?'

'Early twenties, I think. But this illustrates the Ledfields: fondness for children and their sorrow over not having any of their own.'

When Qwilleran phoned the Old Manse to request a tour of the building, he had his strategy planned.

He talked to a cheery individual whom he rightly guessed to be Daisy. Informed when Miss James would be in town, he scheduled an appointment for the day of her absence, saying he was on deadline.

Daisy said she could conduct him through the building the next day.

That evening at eleven P.M. it was Qwilleran's turn to phone Polly with news.

'I'm interviewing Daisy tomorrow. Have you met her?'

'Yes, she's friendlier than the other one. Married to one of the Linguini sons ... Their parents retired from the restaurant business and now live in Florida, although they visit Italy every summer. The sons preferred a party store to a restaurant, and I don't blame them!'

Qwilleran said, 'Their store is the only place I can buy Squunk water by the case, and they deliver!'

'Are you looking forward to visiting the Old Manse, Qwill? I wish, now, that I had accepted Doris Ledfield's invitations . . .'

He said, 'Do you think it's crazy to think that Nathan's grandfather might have have been inspired by Hawthorne's book?'

'Not at all. *Mosses from an Old Manse* was much revered in the days when the house was being built . . .'

'Do you know what I heard today? Nathan's will stipulated that some of his small collectibles should be gradually sold off to provide ongoing funds for child welfare.'

And so it went until it was time for '*À bientôt.*'

He combed *Mosses from an Old Manse* for details that might appear in the Ledfields' Old Manse. He had read the book twice before – once in college and once when he received a copy from the library of the fabulous Agatha Burns.

Agatha was a favorite name in Moose County; after all, the great teacher had lived to be a hundred and had inspired several generations.

Late that evening – after the Siamese were escorted to their quarters on the third balcony, and after Qwilleran had treated himself to a dish of ice cream – he wrote in his journal:

Today I found another clue to the Mystery of the Corrugated Box!

First, I had brought it home from Edd Smith's Place, full of fine old books donated by the Campbells in Purple Point, and Koko went crazy, not over the books but over the box! Why?

Investigation indicated that the Campbells had bought something from the Ledfields, and it came packed in the large brown corrugated box. Now we hear that valuable items are being sold at the bequest of the Ledfield will!

I brought the box from the tool shed, where it sported a do-not-discard sign. I brought it in for Koko's scrutiny, and he went wild again! Why?

The Ledfields had no indoor pets, I'm told. Was there some other kind of aroma that might tickle Koko's whiskers? If so, what?

When I return from my assignment at the Old Manse tomorrow, *will that cat know where I've been?*

Tune in for the next installment.

As he wrote, Qwilleran became aware of thundering paws coming down the ramp from the third balcony. Koko had opened his bedroom door by hanging on the lever-type door handle, a technique he used in emergencies. At the same time Qwilleran heard fire sirens, and from the kitchen window could be seen a pink glow in the dark sky visible above the treetops. Another siren sounded – then another. It sounded like a serious conflagration downtown!

Qwilleran grabbed the phone and called the night desk at the newspaper. 'This is Qwill! Where's the fire?'

'Downtown! The Old Hulk! Can't talk now!' He hung up with a bang.

Qwilleran phoned the McBee farm on the back road, where both the farmer and his brother were volunteer firemen.

Mrs McBee said, 'It's awful! Someone torched the Old Hulk!'

After talking to Mrs McBee, Qwilleran wrote in his journal:

The Old Hulk is a big wooden box on the southwest edge of Pickax with the height of a five-story building and the shape of a coffin. No windows. It was once a depot and warehouse for feed and seed, and

41

farmers came in horse-drawn wagons from three counties to stock up. The interior was a series of lofts connected by ramps. With the advent of paved roads and motor vehicles it was replaced by smaller depots around the county, but the dirty-tan exterior still said FEED AND SEED across the top in letters four feet high, and the eyesore became lovingly known as the Old Hulk. And the stories they tell about it are nothing you would want to tell to your kids and mother-in-law.

Despite the building's appearance and reputation, no one wanted the city to tear it down. But now it has burned down!

Five

Moose County was in shock. Police called it arson. Ruffians from Bixby County had torched the Old Hulk.

Qwilleran went to Lois's Luncheonette for coffee and the public reaction to the disaster. Although the Old Hulk was empty and only the shell of the senior center and could be rebuilt, it was the idea of the crime that rankled. When the newspaper hit the streets, there were statements from city officials, clergy, the donors of the property, retirees, students. Funds would be available to build the Senior Health Club from scratch, but it was the loss of the Old Hulk that hurt. Qwilleran was asked to write a special

Qwill Pen column – consoling, philosophizing, encouraging. At Lois's Luncheonette, the customers were angry and vengeful.

While the public grieved or raged about the arson – as well they might – Qwilleran looked for a constructive approach.

One day while cashing a check at the bank downtown, he stood in line just ahead of Burgess Campbell, lecturer at the local college and revered leader of the Scottish community. Blind from birth, Burgess was always accompanied by his guide dog, Alexander.

Qwilleran said, 'Burgess, do you have a minute to talk? I have a constructive suggestion.'

When their transactions were completed, they met in one of the bank's small conference rooms, and Qwilleran said: 'The K Fund could publish a small book on the Old Hulk, if your students would do some research. They could interview family members, neighbors, public leaders. It would be good experience. They could borrow snapshots and check the photo file at the newspaper. Then a postscript could put a positive slant on the subject by introducing the Senior Health Club.'

Alexander whimpered, and the two men considered that approval. He was a very smart dog.

* * *

Qwilleran had a bad habit of writing a news story before the news broke, or describing a building before it was built. Polly said he should be writing fiction. The products of his imagination always surpassed the actual thing.

As for the Old Manse at Purple Point, Qwilleran wanted to design it to match Hawthorne's book.

And the approach to the mansion signified he might be right . . . There was the iron gate between two rough stone gateposts . . . Then a long, straight driveway between two rows of poplar trees, with beds of daffodils here and there . . . ending at a large building with a prisonlike look: gray brick, plain windows, and a severe entrance door.

The make-believe script ended when he clanged the heavy brass door knocker.

He expected to be admitted by a butler with silver buckles on his shoes, but Daisy Babcock opened the door in a pink pantsuit and a flurry of excitement.

Merrily she said, 'You're Mr Q! Welcome to the Old Manse. Did you bring Cool Koko?'

Only devoted Qwill Pen readers talked nonsense like that. He liked her instantly.

He remembered meeting her at Linguini's Party Store when ordering Squunk water, but her informality came as a shock in a two-story foyer with marble floor, tall mirrors, brocaded walls, a mammoth crystal chandelier, and a stairway as big as the Bridge over the River Kwai.

Soberly, Qwilleran replied, 'Koko regrets that he had a previous appointment with his publisher. He hopes you'll call on him at the barn.'

'I'd love to,' she said. 'Alfredo has told me about it. He makes deliveries of Squunk water, he says.'

'It's a far cry from this little palace. Do you give guided tours?'

'Where would you like to begin?'

'As the King of Hearts said to the White Rabbit, begin at the beginning and keep going till you come to the end. Then stop.'

The loaf-shaped building with modest architecture was one of four wings surrounding a great hall with skylight and a fortune in large oil paintings importantly framed.

There was a music salon with two grand pianos, a dining room that would seat sixteen, and an extensive library upstairs. Every suite had a four-poster bed and an eight-foot highboy.

There was Mrs Ledfield's pride and joy – a large cutting garden that supplied freshly cut flowers for the silver and crystal vases throughout the house ... and there was Nathan Ledfield's specialty: a formal garden of daylilies comprising five varieties compatible with a northern climate.

It was almost as if the Ledfields were still living there. In the music salon there was sheet music open on the racks, as if waiting for the pianist and violinist to make an entrance.

'And this is called the Box Bank,' Daisy said. 'It's not usually shown to anyone outside the family.'

It was a roomful of empty boxes of every size and shape that Nathan had used in buying and selling collectibles: shoe boxes, hatboxes, jewelry boxes, clothing boxes, and large cardboard cartons.

At one point, a young woman in denim came to Daisy and whispered something.

'I'll call him back, Libby. Get his number . . . Did you go to the doctor? I want to know what he said.'

The girl nodded and dashed away.

Daisy said, 'That is our office manager. She went into the garden this morning and was stung by a bee . . . She was Nathan's protégée, you know.'

Altogether, Qwilleran enjoyed coffee and cookies with Daisy more than the extravagances of the Old Manse.

Qwilleran said, 'Your husband is making a delivery from the party store tomorrow. Why don't you come along and say hello to Koko and Yum Yum?'

* * *

Qwilleran described the visit to Polly during their nightly phone call.

'You're a rascal,' she said. 'If Alma Lee James finds out Daisy has visited the barn first, she'll be furious!'

'How do you know?'

'One of the Green Smocks at the bookstore has a cousin who is a housekeeper at the Old Manse, and she says there is jealousy between Daisy and Alma.'

Qwilleran said, 'One of the office personnel came back from the doctor's office while I was there – allergic to a bee sting, they said.'

'Did you know that's how Maggie Sprenkle's husband died? He was working in his rose garden when he was stung and had forgotten his emergency kit. By the time he maneuvered his wheelchair into the house, it was too late. That's why Maggie sold the estate and moved downtown. By the way, what did you think of the Old Manse?'

He said, 'I've decided the Hawthorne connection is too esoteric for Qwill Pen readers. I'm going to leave the Old Manse to the feature writers when the preview takes place. Well . . .

'*À bientôt.*'

'*À bientôt*, dear.'

* * *

Late Thursday afternoon, Koko, who had been invisible for hours, suddenly made an appearance in the kitchen – not to order his dinner but to announce that someone was coming. He jumped on and off the kitchen counter overlooking the barnyard. He was right, of course. In fifteen seconds, according to Qwilleran's stopwatch, the Linguini truck emerged from the wooded trail and drove up to the back door.

Daisy jumped out and looked up at the barn in wonder. Her husband, Fredo, jumped out and started unloading two cases of Squunk water and boxes of cranberry juice, potato chips, pretzels, mixed nuts, and enough wine and spirits to stock the bar for Qwilleran's guests. Koko supervised.

'Is he your new bartender?' Fredo asked.

'No, he's from the State Revenue Department. We have a limited license.'

Daisy was wandering around, gazing up at the ramps, balconies, soaring chimney stacks, and six-foot tapestries hanging from the highest railings.

The Siamese followed her, and Yum Yum allowed her to pick her up while Koko demonstrated his flying-squirrel act, landing on a sofa cushion below.

Then Qwilleran conducted them to the formal foyer with double doors, overlooking the octagonal gazebo screened on all eight sides. It had a view of the butterfly garden, flowering shrubs, and birdhouses on the trail leading to the Art Center on the Old Back Road.

Daisy was reluctant to leave, but they had two more deliveries to make.

Before they left, Qwilleran said, 'It seems to me the Qwill Pen should do a column on vineyards. I've never grown so much as a radish, but grapes appeal to me as – what shall I say? – a satisfying crop.'

'My brother Nick can give you a conducted tour. He's the vintner. Say when!'

On the phone Friday morning, the attorney and Qwilleran plotted Alma Lee's visit to the barn. It would be brief: Bart had another appointment, and Qwilleran had to file his copy for the noon deadline.

When Bart and Alma arrived, the Siamese flew to the loftiest rafters, from which they could observe the first-time visitor.

Qwilleran met them in the parking lot and conducted them to the formal entrance on the other side of the barn.

'Where does this lead?' Alma asked.

'To my mailbox on the back road,' he said, omitting mention of such items as the butterfly pool and the Art Center.

She looked at the screened gazebo. 'Is that where one of your guests shot himself last year?'

'He wasn't a guest; he was an intruder, wanted by the police in three counties,' Qwilleran said, embroidering the truth.

Indoors, she looked up at the balconies and ramps, the large white fireplace cube with stacks rising to the roof forty feet overhead, the six-foot tapestries hanging from balcony railings. 'You could use some small art objects,' she said.

Qwilleran replied, 'The architectural complexities and vast spaces and walls of books don't leave much space for miscellaneous art objects. Apart from that, there's not much to see. It's an atmosphere you *feel*; you don't see it.'

Dropping her critical frown, she said amiably, 'Do you know what I'd like to see in this environment? Large vases filled with fresh flowers! Every area has an ideal spot for it, and you can get fabulous vases from the Ledfield collection in crystal, porcelain, and silver.'

Qwilleran and the attorney exchanged glances.

Qwilleran said, 'With two airborne cats, a vase of flowers would last about ten minutes.'

And Bart said, 'Come, come, Alma. Mr Qwilleran is on deadline at the newspaper.'

Opening her handbag, she found a booklet bound in black and gold. 'Here is the catalog of the Ledfield collection. The items with red stickers are already sold.'

Qwilleran thanked her and gave his wristwatch what was supposed to be a surreptitious glance.

Alma said, 'The most important item has already gone to an old family in Purple Point.'

Barter said, 'We won't have time to sit down, because I have another appointment, and I know you're on deadline, but thanks for showing Alma the interior.'

They were standing – awkwardly, Qwilleran felt – around the area with two large angled sofas.

Suddenly there was a scream as a cat dropped from the rafters onto the cushion of a sofa.

'Sorry,' Qwilleran said to his unnerved guest. 'That's Koko. He wants to be introduced.'

'We don't have time for formalities,' said Barter. 'We're holding up the presses. Thank you, Qwill. Come on, Alma.'

As Barter rushed Alma out of the barn, he looked back and rolled his eyes meaningfully.

As soon as they had driven away, Qwilleran checked the catalog for red-stickered items. He found: a fifteen-inch punch bowl of Chinese export porcelain. It was dated circa 1780. The design was elaborate and historical.

He called Lisa Compton at the ESP. 'Are you still there? Won't they let you go?'

'This sounds like Qwill. Tomorrow's my last day at the bookstore. What can I do for you?'

'About your rich cousins' . . . (Campbell was her maiden name, but she claimed to be from the poor side of the clan) . . . 'Do you happen to know what they bought from the Ledfield estate? Koko's still fascinated by the box the books came in.'

'It was only a punch bowl, they said.'

'Glass or china?'

'China, but quite old. Do you want me to find out the nature of the design? There's no telling what might light a fire under that smart Koko!'

After a little more nonsense common to the fans of 'Cool Koko', the conversation ended.

Qwilleran grabbed the black-and-gold catalog and found the punch-bowl listing: it had sold for sixty thousand dollars.

Six

Six

As Qwilleran had once written in his private journal:

> Anyone who thinks it's easy to write a twice-weekly
> column is misinformed. It may be an enjoyable
> challenge, but it's never easy. Friday has a relentless
> way of following Tuesday, and next Tuesday follows
> this Friday inexorably.

Only the loyalty and enthusiasm of readers kept
Qwilleran's creative juices perking.

The Hawthorne idea had proved to be a 'no-story' – an

unfortunate situation to a newsman with a deadline to meet. He had to resort to his 'trash barrel', as he called the deep drawer of his desk. Postcards from readers, clippings, notes could always be made into a chatty Qwill Pen column with, perhaps, a saying from Cool Koko: 'Faint heart never won the softest cushion in the house.'

Polly said that Qwilleran made the same mistakes over and over again.

But doggedly . . . not stubbornly, he proceeded with another Qwill Pen idea, writing a story in his mind before researching it.

Moose County had a vineyard and a vintner! Qwilleran, Chicago-born, saw his first vineyard in Italy while a young foreign correspondent, and he had retained a romantic impression of the vineyard, the vintner – and perhaps the vintner's daughter.

First he consulted the encyclopedia, determined to avoid another no-story disappointment. He liked the words: *vineyard*, *viticulture*, and *vintner*. He had never wanted to be a farmer, but he wouldn't mind being a vintner. And there was more to viticulture than the making of wine; there were grapes for eating, juice for drinking, raisins for baking, and – his favorite spread for toast – grape jelly. It was an ancient culture, mentioned by Virgil, Homer, and the Bible. Thomas Jefferson tried it. Julia

Ward Howe referred to grapes in 'The Battle Hymn of the Republic'.

Qwilleran had new respect for the Linguini brothers. Nick was the vintner who helped with the store; Alfredo was the storekeeper who helped with the vineyard. He called and made an appointment.

So, on Saturday morning, he drove to the western part of the county, near the lakeshore, and visited Linguini's Party Store. There were quite a few cars in the parking lot. The party store was in a rustic building with a porch running the full width. Indoors, the goods were arranged casually, and the customers were not in a hurry. Some were wandering in and out of a back hall, smiling. It seemed, on investigation, that another homeless pregnant cat had wandered in from the highway and had been given a box and blanket – and had given birth to four minuscule kittens. The smiling customers were putting dollar bills in a pickle jar on the counter for their food, shots, and future expenses.

'Hi, Mr Q,' said Fredo. 'Want to cast your vote for the kittens' names? . . . Nick is expecting you! . . . Marge, ring the vineyard and tell him Qwill is here.'

While waiting for the vintner to come up with his Jeep, Qwilleran accepted compliments from readers, answered questions about Cool Koko's health and happiness, and generally made friends for the *Something*.

As for discovering another two thousand words for the Qwill Pen, however . . . it was another Good Idea That Didn't Work. But he heard some provocative comments from Nick that his sister-in-law, Daisy, had brought home from the Manse; they raised questions.

'Fredo and I think she should quit,' he said. 'Too much monkey business! Know what I mean? There's too much money floating around! Do you realize that a punch bowl sold for sixty thousand? What I'm wondering is, where is the sixty thousand? . . . That young girl who's supposed to be handling Nathan's personal accounts has been whispering suspicions to Daisy. See what I mean?'

Qwilleran agreed it was a sticky situation. 'As I understand it, the entire property has been given to the county. Somebody should blow the whistle! But who? Let me think about it, Nick.'

'Think fast!'

Qwilleran left the vineyard in the firm belief that Koko's curiosity about the large cardboard carton in the shed had some connection with Alma Lee; the cat had dropped from the rafters as if trying to frighten her. Then, when Qwilleran arrived at the barn, he found that the black-and-gold catalog had been torn to shreds!

No sane person would consider this evidence. It was

coincidence, and yet . . . stranger things had happened in connection with Koko! What to do?

While he was downtown with his car, Qwilleran stopped at Grandma's Sweet Shop to pick up ice cream – a gallon of particularly good butter pecan for himself and a quart of vanilla for the Siamese. A real grandmother presided over the cash register in the front, and her grandchildren waited on customers in the rear. Before he could place his order, he saw a waving hand from the seating area (old-fashioned ice-cream tables and chairs of twisted wire). It was Hannah Hawley, wife of Uncle Louie McLeod – with their adopted son, now about nine.

She beckoned to Qwilleran, and as he approached, the young man jumped up and politely added another chair to the table. (This was the waif who had never brushed his teeth or said his prayers when adopted!)

'How's Koko?' she asked. 'I'll never forget his performance at the KitKat Revue.'

'He really blew his cool, didn't he? I think he was expressing an opinion of rhinestone collars.'

Qwilleran inquired, 'How's everything on Pleasant Street?' He signaled for a cup of coffee.

'Pleasant,' she said. 'We're casting for *Cats*. Would you like to try out for Old Deuteronomy?'

'That's about my speed, but if you need a genuine feline, I can supply one.'

'How well we know!' she said. 'By the way, the rehearsal pianist we've had for years has left town, and we were really worried, but we were able to rent Frankie from Lockmaster.'

After two gulps of coffee, Qwilleran asked, 'Would it be naïve to ask who Frankie is – and why he has to be rented?'

'He's crazy,' said Danny.

'Dear, we don't use that word,' he was reprimanded. 'He's an eccentric genius. He can sight-read a musical score he has never seen before! Perfectly! But he'd do it for nothing, and people would take advantage of him, so he's under the management of his family. He's remarkable.'

'What is the family name?' Qwilleran asked.

'His last name is James, but there are lots of Jameses in Lockmaster – like Goodwinters here. All kinds!' She stopped suddenly and looked at the boy. 'Danny, take this money and pay our check at the front counter. Tell Grandma we enjoyed our lunch. And don't forget to count your change.'

When Danny had left on his important mission, Hannah said in a low voice, 'Louie says the Jameses include teachers and preachers, horse breeders, and train robbers. There's an antique shop that we think is way overpriced.

Frankie's managers seem to be a decent sort. They're looking out for his well-being, since he seems to lack a sense of money. He doesn't drive – couldn't get a license, they say . . .' Her voice trailed off as Danny returned to the table with the change. 'We like Frankie, don't we, Danny? He has a friendly, outgoing personality—'

'He has a girlfriend,' Danny interrupted.

Hannah stood up. 'So nice to run into you, Qwill. I'll tell Louie I saw you. Come on, Danny!'

Late that evening Qwilleran and Polly had their eleven P.M. phone chat. He asked, 'Did you have a good day?'

'We had a few interesting customers. Sales were about normal. Dundee ate something he shouldn't have and threw up.'

'I visited Linguini's Party Store. They have a new litter of kittens, and I contributed a name for one of them. I suggested Squunky. Nick showed me around the vineyard. I've decided my interest in vineyards, vintners, and viticulture is purely literary. I like the sound of the words and the quotations from the Bible and poets and playwrights . . . So I'm afraid it's a no-story again . . .'

'Oh dear! You've wasted a lot of time!'

'A writer's time is never wasted. We'll talk about it at dinner Saturday night. How about the Old Grist Mill?

We'll pay the new management the compliment of dressing up.'

Polly hesitated longer than normal. 'Oh, dear! There's a complication . . . You know my friend Shirley in Lockmaster?'

'We haven't met, but I know she's the Lockmaster librarian who quit when you did – and went into book merchandising, the way you did.'

'Yes, but her bookstore is a hundred years old and has been in the family all that time. Saturday is her sixtieth birthday. They're taking a private room at the Palomino Paddock. They want me to be there as a surprise! You're invited, too, but I think you wouldn't enjoy it. They play guessing games.'

'I think you're right.'

'Qwill, I hate to miss our Saturday-night date. It's the first time ever!'

'That's perfectly all right. I'll take Rhoda Tibbitt to dinner and talk about her late husband. Have a good evening. Better not drive back till Sunday morning. I don't want you to drive alone at night.' Then, since he had placed the call, it was his place to say, '*À bientôt.*'

'*À bientôt,*' she said. Did he detect a slight chill on the line? Surely she realized that Rhoda was the eighty-nine-year-old widow of the century-old historian of Moose County.

Polly's defection on Saturday night – in favor of dinner and guessing games in Lockmaster – was just what Qwilleran needed to launch the Tibbitt project. Rhoda was only too happy to cooperate. He picked her up at Ittibittiwassee Estates, where the other residents were thrilled to see one of their number go to dinner with Mr Q.

Qwilleran had made a reservation at Tipsy's Tavern, a roadhouse in a log cabin – with its own poultry farm. It was aptly named for the owner's cat, a portrait of which hung in the main dining room – white with a black patch slipping crazily over one eye. There was a private alcove overlooking the poultry yard that could be closed off for conferences after dinner, and the management was always proud to reserve it for Mr Q.

As for the food, there was no doubt that Tipsy's had the best ham and eggs and chicken à la king in the county – but nothing fancy – and the cook made no claim to being a chef.

Qwilleran said to his guest, 'We'll have dinner first and chat; then we'll clear the table and turn on the recorder.'

He said, 'I first met Homer at the Klingenschoen mansion when it was a museum. The cats and I were living there. Iris Cobb was housekeeper. There was a meeting room upstairs, with an elevator, and Homer was scheduled to speak, but he was late—'

Rhoda nodded and smiled. 'Homer said everyone should have a personal motto, and his was: *Always be late.*'

'Well, there we were, waiting,' Qwilleran said. 'Every time the elevator bell rang, everyone looked at the approaching car. The door would open, and it would be someone else. About the fourth time the bell rang, we all looked at the elevator door, positive that it was Homer. The doors opened, and out walked Koko, with his tail high.'

'I remember,' she said, 'and he seemed surprised that everyone was laughing and shouting.'

'Was Homer a good principal?' Qwilleran asked.

She said, 'We all had a crush on our principal. He was so elegant the way he was dressed and groomed, and he treated his teachers in such courtly fashion. He was the first to retire and went into volunteer work at the Lockmaster Mansion Museum. So when I retired, I went there to apply. Imagine my surprise to find *my principal* in old clothes, crawling around on hands and knees, followed by a belligerent-looking cat! . . . It turned out that the mansion was plagued with mice, and Homer said that it was necessary to find out where they were getting in. He claimed to have found *over a dozen* mouse holes and plugged them up, and the cat was furious because his source of supply was being eroded!

'It was another twelve or fifteen years before we were married, and Homer turned out to be a lot of fun . . . Do you remember the time, Qwill, when a delegation of us in ten limousines rode around the county dedicating bronze plaques?'

'I do indeed! The worse it got, the funnier it got . . . Here comes our dinner. We'll continue the reminiscences later.'

Dinner was served. Chicken, of course, but the conversation never wandered far from the Grand Old Man who had lived to be almost a hundred. There was one question Qwilleran saved until after dessert: 'What can you tell me about the Midnight Marchers?' He turned on the recorder.

'When Homer was nineteen, he used to call on a young lady in the next town – riding there on his bicycle and spending the evening on the porch swing, drinking lemonade and talking. Every half hour, he recalled, her mother came out to the porch to see if they had enough lemonade. At eleven o'clock she suggested that he leave for home, since it was a long ride.

'On one dark night, on the way home, he was mystified

65

to see a long line of small lights weaving across the nearby hills!

'What he did not know – and what it turned out to be – was the annual *ritual* of the Midnight Marchers. They were mourning the loss of thirty-eight miners in a mine disaster that orphaned an entire town.

'Furthermore, it was caused by a greedy mine owner who had failed to take the precautions practiced by competitors . . .

'Every year, the descendants of those orphans donned miners' hats with tiny lights and trudged in silent file across the mine site. They have done it for three generations now, first the sons of orphans, then the grandsons of orphans, and now the great-grandsons. It always made Homer mad as a hatter! He said it was silly schoolboy stuff – putting on miners' hats with lights and staging a spooky pageant. He said they should do something that would benefit the community – and do it in the name of the long-ago victims.'

'How did people react?' Qwilleran asked.

'Oh, he made enemies, who said he was disrespectful of the dead. But as the years went on, the Marchers sounded more and more like a secret society who got together and drank beer. And then Homer got a letter from Nathan Ledfield, that dear man! He said Homer was right. He asked for Homer's help in changing the purpose of the Midnight Marchers without changing the name. Mr Ledfield wanted the Midnight Marchers to benefit orphans. And it proved to be successful.

'The beauty of it is,' said Rhoda, 'that churches and other organizations got behind it, and the Midnight Marchers changed their purpose.'

'Hmmm . . . this sounds vaguely familiar . . .'

'Yes, other philanthropists have copied the Midnight Marchers – not only in Moose County, I believe.'

Qwilleran said, 'Homer must have been pleased to have his lifelong campaign succeed.'

'Yes, but he never wanted any credit.'

Strangely, Qwilleran's mind went to Nathan Ledfield's protégée, but it was getting late, and he saw Rhoda glance at her wristwatch. They returned to Ittibittiwassee Estates.

Seven

Expecting Polly home for Sunday brunch, Qwilleran biked downtown early for the Sunday *New York Times*, unloading such sections as Fashion & Style, Business, Sports, and Classifieds. Otherwise, it would not fit in the basket of his British Silverlight. There were always fellow citizens who were glad to get his leavings.

By the time he returned to the barn, Koko was doing his contortions in the kitchen window, meaning there was a message on the machine.

It would be Polly, he knew, announcing her arrival and making plans for the day . . . Instead, when Qwilleran pressed the button, the voice was that of Wetherby Goode: 'This is Joe. Polly called and asked me to give her cats their breakfast. She said to tell you she won't be home till late afternoon.'

Qwilleran fortified himself with a cup of coffee and dialed the weatherman. He said, 'Appreciate the message, Joe. Did she mention what was happening in that jungle down there?'

'Just what I was going to ask you, pal.'

'She went to a dinner last night, leaving her cats on the automatic feeder and expecting to drive back this morning for the usual Sunday activities. No telling what changed her mind.'

'Anything can happen south of the border.'

'You should know, Joe.' (He was a native of Horseradish down there.) 'Polly went to a birthday party for a friend who was library director of Lockmaster but left to manage the family bookstore.'

'Sure, I know the store. Bestbooks. It's been there forever. Why weren't you invited?'

'I was, but I declined. They play guessing games at their parties.'

'I know what you mean . . .'

'Stop in for a snort on your way to your broadcast tomorrow and I'll fill you in – on who won.'

* * *

During this conversation, the Siamese had sat side by side, quietly awaiting developments. He gave them a good brushing with the silver-backed hairbrush . . . then played a few rounds of the necktie game . . . then announced, 'Read!' Koko leaped to the bookshelf and knocked down *The Portrait of a Lady*. It had more gilt on the spine, he observed, than others that had come in the last purchase.

The first chapter was interrupted by the phone – and the comfortable voice of Mildred Riker, inviting him to an afternoon repast with the Rikers. 'But I can't find Polly,' she said. 'She wasn't at church.'

'She's out of town,' Qwilleran explained.

'Then you come, and I'll invite someone from the neighborhood.'

When he arrived an hour later, he was glad to see Hixie Rice, promotion director for the *Something*.

'Where's Polly?' she asked.

'In Lockmaster – probably up to no good. Where's Dwight?'

'In the same place, probably for the same reason.'

Drinks were served on the deck. They talked about the Old Hulk. The Scottish community was prepared to underwrite a new building. Volunteer carpenters, electricians, and painters were offering their services, proud to have

71

their names on an honor roll in the lobby of the building.

The meal was served indoors, as usual.

Mildred said, 'I envy Qwill's screened gazebo. He can serve outdoors, and the cats can be out there without leashes.'

After dessert (peach cobbler with crème fraîche and pecans) the two men entertained with their favorite topic: growing up in Chicago. Hixie had not heard the story before.

Mildred said, 'Tell about summer camp.'

The oft-told tale went like this:

QWILL: 'My father died before I was born, and so Mr Riker functioned as dad for both of us – taking us to the zoo and parades, giving advice, discussing our report cards, getting us out of scrapes.'

ARCH: 'One year he decided we should go to summer camp and learn something useful like doing the Australian crawl, rigging a sailboat, climbing a tree, whittling a wood whistle . . .'

QWILL: 'But there's only one thing we remember. Every night we'd sit around a campfire, listen to stories, and sing camp songs loudly, but not well.'

ARCH: 'But the only thing that either of us remembers in detail is the campfire chant.'

QWILL: 'Not only do we remember every word, but it runs through the mind at the most inopportune times.'

ARCH: '—Like, when facing a traffic judge.'

QWILL: '—or getting married.'

ARCH: '—Would you like a performance?'

Hixie squealed, 'Please do!'

The two men sat up in their chairs, eyed each other for a cue, then launched into a loud, bouncy beat:

'Away down yonder not so very far off
A jaybird died of the whooping cough.
He whooped *so hard with the whooping cough*
That he whooped *his head and his tail*
Right off!'

There was a moment's silence, during which Polly always said, 'To quote Richard the Third, I am amazed.'

Hixie squealed, 'I love it! I wanta learn it!'

'Want to hear the second verse?' they asked. 'It's the same as the first.'

The party broke up at a sensible hour, and Qwilleran drove home to get up-to-date on Polly's escapade. He would ask her:

How was the party?

Were there sixty candles on the cake?

Who was there?

Were they dressed bookish or horsey?

Did they really play guessing games?

Who won?

What were the prizes?

What church do they attend?

How was the preacher?

He was a thorough interviewer, and she liked to be interviewed.

When he arrived at the barn, the cat-in-the-window message assured Qwilleran that someone had checked in. It was the weatherman.

'Polly's home, but she's beat! Call me, not her. She looked frazzled, Qwill, high on excitement, short on sleep. I told her to turn in and I'd notify you.'

Qwilleran said, 'She never drinks more than half a glass of sherry. She's known Shirley for years!'

'Yeah, but . . . something got her overexcited and maybe it interfered with her sleep. Too bad she had to drive home alone. We'll keep in touch. Don't worry.'

That evening, around eleven o'clock, Qwilleran was

reading in his lounge chair, and the cats were sprawled on his lap. Suddenly Koko was alerted! He looked at the desk phone. And it rang. It was Polly, reporting for their bedtime chat.

'Qwill!' she cried. 'I suppose you wonder what happened to me. I've never been so exhausted in my life! A cup of cocoa, a few hours' sleep with my cuddly cats, and I revivified . . . I hope you didn't worry about me.'

'We'll go to dinner tomorrow night, and you can fill me in.'

'I'll have something exciting to tell you,' Polly said.

'Give me a hint.'

'No hints. If you guess what it is, it won't be a surprise . . . *À bientôt!*'

'*À bientôt.*'

Eight

On his way to the radio station, Wetherby Goode often stopped at Qwilleran's barn for a pick-me-up, and the newsman enjoyed his impromptu visits – not only to get the inside track on the weather but to share neighborly news, and the neighbors at the Willows were always making news. Joe had been genuinely concerned about Polly.

When he arrived at the kitchen door and dropped on a stool at the bar, he was greeted by Koko and Yum Yum, who would not be surprised to receive a friendly cat snack from Jet Stream.

Qwilleran poured and said, 'Well, she survived!'

'She's a tough one! Never underestimate the power of a cup of cocoa!'

The male cat jumped to the bar top, hearing his name.

Qwilleran said, 'I expect to hear the whole story when we have dinner tonight. The problem is: Monday is not a good night for dining out. The Mackintosh Inn is too formal, the Grist Mill too festive, the Boulder House too far.'

'Why not get a picnic supper catered by Robin O'Dell, Qwill, and serve it in the gazebo? You don't know how lucky you are to have premises that are screened.'

Qwilleran said, 'Once in a while you come up with a good idea . . . Have another splash in your glass.'

'And if there's anything Polly doesn't know about those horse people in Lockmaster, call on me. I can give you some ancient history about Bestbooks, Qwill. It's been in the same family for a hundred years, you know. At one time they kept a bottle in the back room and had a men's club back there. Lots of loud laughter and bawdy jokes. Parents put the whole store off-limits to kids. Women wouldn't go in to buy a cookbook. They lost a lot of business to mail order and secondhand and the public library.'

Qwilleran said, 'The librarians of both Lockmaster and

Pickax became great friends at that time. That's why Polly was invited to Shirley's birthday party yesterday.'

Joe drained his glass and headed for the back door.

'Before you go, Joe, one question. Does Jet Stream accept food from the automatic feeder?'

'He'll take anything he can get . . . Why?'

'When Koko hears the little bell ring and sees the little door open, he looks at the food in disbelief and then looks up at me and shakes his right paw – then sniffs the dish again and shakes his other paw before walking away.'

There was time, before Polly came from the bookstore, to call Celia and order a picnic supper.

Celia said, 'Does she like cold soup? I have some lovely gazpacho. And I have individual quiches in the oven with bacon and tomato. For dessert, chilled Bartlett pears would be nice, with a bit of Stilton . . . Pat can deliver it after five o'clock, and I'll send a little goodie for the cats.'

When Polly drove to the barn around six o'clock, Qwilleran said, 'We'll have an aperitif in the gazebo. Will you take the cats?'

She knew right where to go for their 'limousine', a canvas tote bag in the broom closet, advertising the Pickax Public Library. Qwilleran carried a tray with sherry for her and Squunk water for himself. 'I want to hear all about the Birthday Party of the Century.'

'Well!' she said, promising a momentous report. 'You wouldn't have liked it, Qwill. The main dining room looked like a stable – tack hanging on the walls, waitresses in riding boots – everything but the horses! I thought the food was terrible! I ordered salmon; I don't know what they did to it.'

Parodying an old joke, Qwilleran said, 'Apart from that, Mrs Duncan, how did you like the party?'

'There were forty guests at long institutional tables . . . forty frosted cupcakes, each with a tiny candle, and a matchbook . . . forty gift-wrapped birthday presents, including one that must have been a refrigerator and one that was obviously a bicycle!'

'How did the guest of honor react?'

'Shirley is always charming. She told her son she would like everything trucked to her home – where she could open the small ones with her shoes off and her cat on her lap. She said she would send everyone a thank-you note suitable for framing. That means an original cartoon.'

'Shirley sounds like a clever woman. I'm sorry I never met her . . . What about the guessing games? You haven't mentioned them.'

'They were boring: Why does the firefly flash his light?

Who owns the Volvo company in Sweden? Who explored Idaho in the early nineteenth century?'

· They were both accustomed to Literary Club questions. Who wrote these lines: 'She walks in beauty like the night . . .' 'Tomorrow, and tomorrow, and tomorrow, creeps in this petty pace from day to day . . .' 'Order is a lovely thing, on disarray it lays its wing.'

'The best part of the evening was the music. A young man played fabulous piano! Pop and classical. A young woman turned pages for him. They say she's also his chauffeur – or is it chauffeuse? He has some kind of disability and can't drive. He's also a piano tuner. He tuned Doris's piano at the Old Manse four times a year, including regulating and voicing. Mostly he plays piano for hire.'

When Polly stopped for breath he asked, 'Is his name Frankie? I believe he's rehearsal pianist for the production of *Cats*. All very interesting.'

Later Qwilleran asked about Shirley's ideas for a bookstore.

'Bestbooks and Pirate's Chest had entirely different problems. *They* had a hundred-year-old building with a boozy aroma in the rear and a questionable reputation – not to mention bad plumbing. With Shirley's know-how and ideas and an unlimited budget, Bestbooks was born again. Her first move was to hire a bibliocat, a brother of Dundee,

81

and customers' frowns changed to smiles. Then, just as we have an actual pirate's chest hanging on the wall, Shirley introduced a favorite work of art . . . Are you familiar with the Rodin sculpture *The Thinker*?'

Qwilleran had never seen it but knew its pose: male model, seated, with fist on chin and elbow on knee.

'Shirley has never seen the original, either, but she has a photo enlarged and framed as a focal point of the store. Obviously it represents "Thinking, not drinking." And then a competition among customers named the official cat Thinker – a wonderful name for a feline.'

He said, 'I'm sorry I don't know Shirley. What's she like?'

'She has a commanding figure and is very pleasant. Just don't call her *Shirl*, that's all!'

Qwilleran said, 'There's something on your mind, Polly. It's been bothering you ever since Shirley's party. Would you like to unload?'

She looked relieved. 'How to begin . . . At the end of the dinner, Shirley's son, Donald, who has been functioning as president of Bestbooks, made a very touching speech about Shirley and how she gave up a library career three years ago to save a century-old bookstore that had been going downhill. In the last three years, Shirley's personality and brainpower have tripled the annual income.

For that reason the Bestbooks board of directors have voted Shirley a bonus: something she has always wanted – a trip to Paris. Shirley screamed – something she never does. Then Donald said that all expenses would be paid – *for two!* Shirley looked at me, and I screamed! Then we clutched each other and both cried.'

Qwilleran was stunned into silence but recovered to say, 'I'm very happy for you, Polly!'

She said, 'I only wish you were going with me.'

'So do I, dear.'

Polly said, 'At least I won't have to impose on neighbors and worry about Brutus and Catta. They can stay at Pet Plaza, and Judd Amhurst can manage the bookstore.'

She added, 'A Lockmaster travel agent will handle airline tickets, hotel reservations, and sightseeing.'

Later that evening, and in the days that followed, Qwilleran speculated that they could have been traveling about the globe together. Why had they both allowed themselves to be trapped in the workaday world? Now there was no telling whom Polly would meet. There had been that professor in Canada, that antiques dealer in Williamsburg, those attorneys and architects at the K Fund in Chicago.

And now there were all those Frenchmen! She liked men, and they were attracted to her agreeable manner, resulting from a lifetime career in a public library. Her musical voice might be interpreted as being seductive. She had a beautiful complexion – the result, she said, of eating broccoli and bananas. She dressed attractively – with individual touches of her own design. Altogether, Polly seemed too young for the silver in her hair. And when she entered a room wearing a Duncan plaid over the shoulder, pinned with a silver cairngorm . . . she stopped conversation.

And now those two likable and attractive women were going to Paris!

Nine

The next day, a Tuesday, Qwilleran met his Qwill Pen deadline but felt an underlying disappointment, although he kept telling himself to snap out of it. Everywhere he went, the entire population of Pickax seemed to know that Polly was going to Paris without him.

One conference was with Lisa Compton, who wanted to update him on the proposed program at the Senior Health Club. When given a choice of venue, she gladly chose the barn.

'How's your crotchety and lovable husband?' he asked. Lyle was superintendent of schools.

'Crotchety and lovable, in that order,' she said cheerfully.

They decided it was too good a day to sit anywhere but the gazebo.

He asked, 'Is there anything the Qwill Pen can do for you?'

'That's for you to decide, Qwill. I'll tell you where we stand. The building itself is progressing incredibly fast. With all-volunteer labor. We're selling memberships and collecting ideas for activities. I've never seen this town so excited. The wonderful thing is that they want to learn how to do things! Does the Qwill Pen have any suggestions?'

'As a matter of fact, yes! I've been thinking about it – and about the pleasure I get from writing a private journal. It's not like a diary, where you record daily events – but a place for thoughts and ideas, no matter how personal or crazy. No matter how amateurish, it's something to leave to future generations – something that will be appreciated. I'd be willing to introduce the idea, give a few tips – even read some of my own entries.'

'Qwill! This is more than I expected! You could introduce the idea now – in the community hall, and get them started. Is there anything I should be doing?'

'Just tell the stationer to lay in a good supply of ordinary school notebooks with lined pages.'

* * *

That night as Qwilleran sat down to write in his private journal, he had a flashback to his lean and hungry years as a young man in New York. He wrote:

My furnished room had an old windup Victrola and a single 78 record: Johnny Mercer singing 'I'm gonna sit right down and write myself a letter.' I played it every night because I couldn't afford to buy another one.

Now, three decades later, it runs through my mind every night when I sit down to write to myself in my journal.

Qwilleran's phone rang frequently the following day.

'Is it true about Polly?'

'Why aren't you going?'

'Why Paris?'

'Does she speak French?'

'Are you giving a big party?'

'How long will she be gone?'

Finally he remembered the advice of his childhood mentor: 'When fed up, take the bull by the horns.'

He went downtown to Lanspeak's Department Store and asked Carol about a going-away gift for Polly. 'Not another scarf! And certainly not a bottle of French perfume!'

She said, 'We have a wonderful travel coat – gabardine – with snap flaps on the patch pockets – with secret pockets in the lining – and a brimmed rain hat. Polly looked at it but thought the price a little steep.'

'I'll take it!' he said. 'In fact, I'll take two. Is there a choice of colors?'

Now, it seemed to Qwilleran, would be a good time to work on his senior program for Lisa Compton. It would be easy. He could tell an anecdote or two about Cool Koko . . . then show a stack of the school notebooks he filled with journal entries. Never a day went by without filling a page.

On some days there were brief entries:

When Yum Yum, my female Siamese, has access to a long hallway with many doors to bedrooms, bathrooms, etc., her performance is a wonder to watch. The doors are open; the rooms are unoccupied much of the time.

With stiff legs and resolute steps, she proceeds to walk the length of the hall down the exact center, looking straight ahead. At each open door she stops in her tracks; her body remains motionless except for her head, which swivels to look in the room. Only her eyeballs move as she appraises the interior. Then, finding nothing of interest, she switches her head back to the main course and trudges on to the next open door.

I have never seen her find anything of interest, but she continues her silent inspections.

There are times when I would like to redesign this barn and put the front door in the front and the back door in the back. But what is the back? And what is the front?

I stable my bicycles in the elegant foyer – and greet guests at the kitchen door.

I guess this is what happens when you convert a drive-through apple barn into a residence. And it reminds me of the pioneers who founded Pickax. Did they have a mischievous sense of humor when they put North Street south of South Street . . . and when they put storefronts facing the alley and loading docks facing the street?

Pickax is the quintessential absurdist city!

That evening, Qwilleran phoned the Comptons and told Lisa he was ready to talk to the seniors about private journals. He had some free time. He would read a couple of his own entries. They could start their own journals without waiting for the Senior Health Club to be finished.

Lisa said they would announce the date at the community hall.

'There'll be a crowd!' she said. 'We'll notify the Traffic Department.'

On Thursday, Qwilleran felt the need for lunch and camaraderie with Kip MacDiarmid. The editor in chief of the *Lockmaster Ledger* was one of his best friends, and Kip's wife, Moira, was the marmalade breeder who had presented the affable Dundee to the Pirate's Chest. Their favorite restaurant was in the old Inglehart mansion.

Kip's first words were, 'Moira says you and Polly must come to dinner soon.'

'Polly's leaving for Paris for two weeks,' Qwilleran said, 'with Shirley Bestover.'

When told the particulars, Kip asked, 'Who's planning their trip?'

'It appears there's a semiretired travel agent in Lockmaster, who will go along to see that they get the best of everything.'

'Him, I know him! He's an old roué, but I suppose Polly and Shirley can handle him. You might tip them off.'

They talked about many things. 'If you would syndicate your column in the *Ledger*, we'd run it on page one and it would double our circulation . . .'

'Want to know something, Kip? Our office manager at the paper says that most of the mail that comes addressed to Koko has a Lockmaster postmark . . . You've got a bunch of Koko-nuts around here.'

They mentioned the local election that was coming up. 'The incumbent is sure to win,' Kip said. 'The challenger is confident, but . . . as the saying goes, he couldn't get elected dogcatcher!'

Then Kip made a suggestion that launched Qwilleran like a rocket. It was just what he needed under the present circumstances. 'Were you ever involved in the Theater of the Absurd?'

'Yes, I was in New York and saw it at its best. I always wanted to write an absurdist play, but never did.'

'There's talk about a revival. Would you be interested?' Kip asked.

'How about an original absurdist creation? How about: *The Cat Who Was Elected Dogcatcher*?'

Then Kip changed the subject slyly: 'Moira wants me to ask you if you're still practicing medicine without a license. You could bottle this stuff and sell it.'

He referred to a humorous verse Qwilleran had composed for his last birthday. He brought a card from his vest pocket printed with a typical Qwilleran limerick:

An editor known as Kip
Is said to run a tight ship.
His heart is large,
He's always in charge,
But he won't take any lip.

The editor said, 'Whenever I'm feeling below normal, physically or otherwise, I read your prescription and it gives me a boost.'

Qwilleran said, 'I've been thinking of writing a book on the subject of humorous verse—'

'Do it! I'll buy the first copies and give them to all my friends.'

As they talked, Qwilleran's gaze was prone to wander across the room to a table where three women were lunching in unusual hats.

He remarked, 'Polly would go for those bizarre hats, and she could wear one well.'

The editor corrected him. 'Moira says they're called art hats.'

'I beg everyone's pardon' was the facetious apology. 'Do you know the women who're wearing them? They keep looking over here at us.'

'They're looking at your moustache. They all know who you are. They see your photo in the Qwill Pen on Tuesdays and Fridays . . . I still think you should syndicate it to the *Ledger*.'

'Pleasant thought, but it wouldn't work.' He grabbed the check when it came to the table. 'My treat. Tell Moira she can invite us to dinner when Polly gets back.'

The editor left, and Qwilleran signed the check and left a tip, noting that two art hats had left the room, and the other woman was still eyeing his moustache.

On the way out of the restaurant he said to the hostess, 'I'm embarrassed. I know that woman at the fireplace table, but I can't place her.'

The hostess's face brightened. 'There are usually three. The public library is closed on Thursday, and they call themselves the Librarians Who Lunch. That one is Vivian Hartman, the chief librarian.'

She looked very pleasant when he approached. Her hat, he noted, was brimmed and about a foot in diameter . . . two shades of velvet, and a large silk sash with a realistic peony.

'I beg your pardon, are you Miss Hartman? I'm Jim Qwilleran from the *Moose County Something*.'

'Yes, I know! Won't you sit down?' she answered, and he pulled up a chair.

'I must say I admire the hats you ladies wear.'

'We make them ourselves . . . in memory of your

Thelma Thackeray. Her brother Thurston had a veterinary hospital here. We're still grieving over both of them. Not to mention her loss of twenty-five art hats.' She looked for his reaction.

He nodded somberly. 'Did you know that they had been photographed just before the calamity?'

'No!' she exclaimed. 'No one in Lockmaster knew!'

'Our photographer was commissioned, and I went along to hold his lights. I could show you a set of glossy prints – if you would come for lunch at my barn next Thursday,' he said. 'Thelma had commissioned a California woman to write a book, but she lost interest when the hats were destroyed . . . Perhaps . . .'

'Yes . . . perhaps,' the librarian said, 'we might revive the idea.'

Ten

As F Day approached, Polly became more distracted. There was no time for dining at fine restaurants followed by a classical concert on the magnificent music system of Qwilleran's barn. She spent her days instructing Judd and Peggy to take over the Pirate's Chest in her absence. She spent her evenings making packing lists, reading about Paris, brushing up on her college French, having long telephone conversations with Shirley Bestover; Qwilleran felt left out. His offers of 'any kind of assistance' were appreciated but apparently unneeded.

* * *

That evening and in those to come, Qwilleran took the initiative to phone at eleven P.M., knowing that Polly would be distracted with last-minute considerations of all kinds. She had not yet told him when she was leaving, and he stubbornly refused to ask. He said not a word about his Theater of the Absurd project (she had always despised that kind of play) or the Librarians Who Lunch.

Polly told him, 'Wetherby Goode will take Brutus and Catta to the Pet Plaza and visit them twice a week. Isn't that thoughtful of him? Dr Connie will water my plants and take in my mail. We have such wonderful neighbors at the Willows.' (Qwilleran had no comment.)

She said, 'There's a five-hour difference in time between Paris and Pickax, dear, so we'll have to forgo our late-night chats.'

'I'll give you a pocket recorder to take along, and you can dictate a running account of your adventures to bring home.'

He told her, 'If any problems arise in Paris, don't hesitate to contact me collect – at any hour of the day or night, regardless of time differential.'

When his parting gifts were delivered (blue gabardine for her, khaki gabardine for Shirley), the two women were overwhelmed. It was not until they had left for the Lockmaster airport in Shirley's son's limousine that

Qwilleran felt at ease again, and not even lonely! After all, he had Koko and Yum Yum for companions, two columns a week to write for the newspaper. He was committed to deadline on Homer Tibbitt's biography. He was working on his program for the Senior Health Club, to be given at the community hall since the redesigned building was far from complete. Also, the Literary Club's visiting lecturer on Proust was scheduled to be his overnight guest at the barn. (He was said to be an ailurophile, so Koko's aerial demonstrations would be amusing, not threatening.) Plus, to write a play in the absurdist style. All this . . . and Polly would be gone only two weeks!

Later that evening Qwilleran called Kip MacDiarmid at home. 'Were you serious about my writing an absurdist play?'

'I think it would be a hoot,' Kip replied.

'Would you use the title I suggested?' Qwilleran asked.

'Why not? When can you do it?' Kip asked.

'I've just done it; it took half an hour. I'll send it to your office by motorcycle messenger in the morning.'

THE CAT WHO GOT
ELECTED DOGCATCHER

A Play in One Act by Jim Qwilleran

CAST

Man with dog on leash

Woman with cat in arms

Street sweeper with broom

SCENE

A park with trees painted on background . . . park bench in bright green, center front . . . trash barrel overflowing in rear.

WOMAN (to cat in arms): Stop complaining, Jerome! If I put you down in the wet grass, you'll only want to be picked up again.

Enter MAN (with dog tugging on leash): No, Eugene, it's against the law. (Sees woman.) Oh, hi! Hi!

WOMAN: Hi!

MAN: Is that Jerome? I thought he skipped town after the . . . incident.

WOMAN: He came back.

MAN: Does he have any means of support?

WOMAN: His constituents are raising a slush fund.

MAN: Is that what he eats?

WOMAN: He'll eat anything.

MAN: He looks as if he eats better than I do.

WOMAN: Do you have time to sit down?

MAN: They just painted the benches.

WOMAN: That was last week.

They both sit . . . and look surprised.

WOMAN: Oh, well, I wasn't going anywhere. How about you?

MAN: I had an appointment at the traffic court.

CAT: Yeowwww!

WOMAN: You're sitting on his tail.

MAN: Has the candidate ever held office?

WOMAN: Only as ratcatcher.

MAN: Why did he quit?

WOMAN: No reason.

MAN: What makes you think he could catch dogs?

CAT: Yeowwww!

WOMAN: See? He's quite confident.

MAN: I'm still sitting on his tail!

WOMAN: Jerome! The gentleman has offered to be
   your campaign manager!

CAT: (Hisses at man.)

WOMAN: Jerome! This gentleman is here to get you
   votes!

100

MAN: Frankly, I don't think his name is suitable for public office.

WOMAN: What would you suggest? Pussy?

MAN: I had in mind something strong like Tiger . . . OUCH!

WOMAN: Jerome! That's politically incorrect!

MAN: I'm not sure he's qualified.

WOMAN: Jerome! Behave! . . . He hasn't had his lunch. He knows you have a sandwich in your pocket.

MAN: It's only peanut butter.

WOMAN: He'll eat anything except spinach.

MAN: (Attempts to leave in defense of his sandwich.)

All three are stuck.

The End

That night Qwilleran added to his private journal:

Well, she's gone. There was no send-off. She just faded away. It would have been different if I were living at the Willows. But the weather's much too good at the barn. Carol Lanspeak said that the two mature women probably looked like the Bobbsey Twins with their blue and khaki outfits. Tonight I watched Koko at eleven o'clock to see if he expected a call. He ignored the phone. He knew she was on her way to France . . . if not already there!

When the Linguini Party Store truck delivered another supply of Squunk water and other treats, Qwilleran was pleased to see Daisy Babcock step out of the passenger side. She was waving a camera.

'Libby Simms at the Old Manse wants me to take a picture of Koko. She memorizes everything you write about him. I told her you wouldn't mind.'

'True! But Koko will mind. Whenever a camera is pointed in his direction, he crosses his eyes, bares his fangs, and scratches his ear . . . But go ahead. They're both in the gazebo.'

He helped Alfredo unload.

'I see your wife is still working at the Old Manse.'

'Can't pry her away from that place.'

'No more bee stings?'

'Well, the girl with the allergy is supposed to take a medical kit every time she goes in the garden, which is several times a day, and she forgets, so Daisy bought her a hospital jacket with big pockets in a bright color to hang just inside the garden door. She just grabs it when she goes out. The kit is in the pockets . . . That's the way my wife is – always thinking of solutions to problems . . . How long before you move back to the condo?'

'It depends on the weather. The leaves haven't even started to turn,' Qwilleran marveled . . . He walked around to the gazebo and found the two cats on Daisy's lap.

'No problem,' she said. 'Are you trying out for the *Cats* musical?'

'No, but I'll attend a couple of rehearsals, looking for cues for the Qwill Pen. I hear Libby's boyfriend is a terrific piano player.'

'Did you know he was the Ledfields' piano tuner? They're a darling couple.'

Then Alfredo appeared, and the party was over.

In preparation for the evening, Qwilleran gave the Siamese an early dinner, and they walked around it three times as if questioning the propriety of the timing. For himself he ordered soup, sandwich, and pie from Robin O'Dell Catering.

To get in the mood for the *Cats* rehearsal Qwilleran played a recording of the musical and was half wishing he were singing a role, when . . . he heard a sound that made the hair stand up on the back of his neck. It was Koko's death howl!

Starting with an abdominal guttural, it ascended through the cat's stiffened body and ended with a curdling shriek!

Qwilleran had heard it before, and it meant that . . . someone, somewhere was the victim of murder!

He mopped his brow as he considered the possibilities.

He phoned the city desk at the *Something*. 'Qwill here. Any foul play reported?'

'No, but someone died as the result of a bee sting. Bad scene. Must've been allergic. My kids are getting stung all the time.'

Later in the evening Qwilleran attended the *Cats* rehearsal at the community hall. (The new music center was still being adapted from a public school.) The McLeods' nine-year-old adopted son, Danny, considered himself in charge of the rehearsal: arranging chairs, handing out scores, asking if anyone wanted a drink of bottled water, asking Qwilleran if he wanted something to write on.

When Uncle Louie mounted the podium and rapped on the music stand with his baton, the nine-year-old ushered the singers into the proper sections. No one seemed to find the boy at all too young for the responsibility.

However . . . the grimness of the conductor's expression and the presence of a substitute pianist quieted the assembly quickly. When he had everyone's attention, he said, somberly, 'A fatal accident has robbed our pianist of his assistant and robbed our group of a cheerful and valued member. Libby Simms. Let us express our sorrow and sympathy by standing for a few minutes of silence.'

The chorusers stood, and Hannah, at the piano, played 'Amazing Grace'.

Qwilleran, glancing around the assembly of stunned singers, caught Daisy's eye; the men in her family were trying out for roles. She motioned toward the exit, and when he met her in the hallway, her face looked taut.

She said, 'Qwill, I've got to talk to you.'

They found a bench near the drinking fountain.

'A sad story,' he said. 'I thought she had an emergency medical kit.'

'She was supposed to keep it in a pocket of the jacket – I got hot pink, her favorite color. She sometimes wore the jacket when she went on dates with Frankie. She was young and forgot to check the pockets. It's hard to convince young people to be careful.'

'Has the kit turned up since the tragedy?' he asked.

'I don't know. I've been too upset to think straight. Fredo thought it would do me good to come to the rehearsal with him and Nick ... but ...' She burst into tears again ...

Qwilleran gave her a small packet of tissues.

When Daisy's sobs subsided, she said, 'Fredo's right! I've got to get away from that place.'

'You have talents and personality that would be useful in the exciting community that Nathan has left us. It would please him if you were a part of it. Let me look into it for you. Think of it as the beginning of something, not the end of something.'

One evening Qwilleran phoned his longtime friend John Bushland at home. 'Bushy, do you still have the negatives of Thelma Thackeray's hats that you and I slaved over?'

The photographer, who was losing his hair rapidly, liked to thumb his nose at his misfortune with an impudent nickname.

'Sure thing! Why do you ask?'

'I have an idea for a public-library exhibit in two counties that would be good public relations all around. K

Fund will sponsor. But first, can I get a set of prints before Thursday? Eight-by-ten color prints. How they would be presented – will come later.'

'Sure thing!'

Bushy was always cooperative. And he and Qwilleran had shared experiences that had cemented their friendship – with one reservation: Qwill would never again go out on Bushy's powerboat!

Eleven

While Qwilleran waited for Polly's first postcard from Paris, imagine his surprise at receiving a letter!

Dear Qwill,
It's our first day here, and something funny happened that's too good to keep!

Shirley wanted to take a nap, and our travel agent went looking for a bar. I just wanted to walk around and pinch myself. Was I really in Paris?

I was standing on a kerb, waiting to cross the street, when a short middle-aged man came up to me.

He was wearing a T-shirt with a large American flag on the chest – and carrying a French-English phrase book. He pointed to one translation and read slowly.

'Pardonnez-moi. Où se trouve l'opéra?'

I couldn't resist the cliché: 'I don't know. I'm a stranger here myself,' I said.

Instead of being amused, he was obviously embarrassed, because he virtually fled from the scene. Too bad. It would have been fun to find out where he was from – Chicago? Denver?

Actually, I was flattered that he mistook me for a native! The Parisiennes have a definite chic!

And I've never seen such beautiful postcards!

Love from Polly

P.S. What made it so funny – I was wearing my blue gabardine coat and hat from Lanspeak's.

Wednesday morning, G. Allen Barter arrived for legal business at the barn, whistling 'Memory' from the musical *Cats*.

Qwilleran said, 'Don't tell me. You're singing Grizabella in *Cats*? I would have thought you were more the Rum Tum Tugger type.'

'Not guilty! My wife and I took our eldest to the tryouts. We saw you there, but you didn't sing. Did you get cold feet?'

When the bantering was over and the two men had trooped to the conference area with two tail-happy cats and a tray of coffee, Qwilleran said, 'Does the county still need a coordinator for community activities?' Where once there had been only a community hall and athletic field, bequests from old families had now made it feasible for a music center, a senior club, and two museums as well. And although the office of HBB&A had handled the transition, the time had come for citizen control.

Qwilleran said to Bart, 'Daisy Babcock has the intelligence, skills, and creativity to handle it. I suggest you call her to come in for an interview. The K Fund will back me up.'

'What does Koko say about it?' Bart joshed.

'He was the one who suggested it.'

There was the usual amount of joking and coffee swigging, followed by serious decision making and document signing. Then Qwilleran broke the news.

'How would the K Fund like to undertake a little two-county collaboration? That is, share an exhibit that has warm ties to both of them! We're usually competing, criticizing, or opposing in some way.'

After a pause to arouse Bart's curiosity, Qwilleran continued: 'I think you will remember that Moose County twins once returned to the north country in later life. Thelma Thackeray had a career in Hollywood; Thurston Thackeray had made a name for himself, in providing medical services for the horses and dogs of Lockmaster. The passing of the two wonderful people was deeply mourned and – because of questionable circumstances – not properly honored.'

He stopped for breath, and his listener was interested.

'The activity would center about the bookstore of Pickax and the library of Lockmaster, and there would be newspaper features and talks. The twins' father is buried in a hilltop grave, with a simple grave-marker inscription: *Milo the potato farmer*. Some believe he was a bootlegger.'

Bart said, 'Go ahead! Anything that launches the two counties in one direction will be okayed in Chicago.'

Qwilleran said, 'We'll start with the photo exhibit at the two locations. Research, newspaper coverage, talks, et cetera, will come later. Everyone will want to jump on the bandwagon.'

That evening Qwilleran received a surprise phone call from Judd Amhurst. The temporary manager of the bookstore said, 'Wouldn't you know the showcases arrived today! Polly's been expecting them for weeks . . . no, months! As soon as she left the country they arrived!' It was like this. The bookstore architects had designed a space for exhibits of a cultural nature.

Qwilleran asked, 'Did you and Polly plan exhibits in them?'

'We had lots of ideas, but perhaps you'd like to make some suggestions. Showcases, too. They're really elegant.'

'Good, I'll drop in at the bookstore tomorrow.' Qwilleran was a welcome visitor at the Pirate's Chest . . . and not simply because he always brought a box of treats from Grandma's Sweet Shop.

That night Qwilleran wrote in his private journal:

These are busy days in Moose County: new ideas, new activities, new people. And the same old gossips in the coffeehouses. They are not always right, but they are always provocative. And the best place to listen to the best scuttlebutt is Lois's Luncheonette downtown. The trick is . . . to listen without getting involved. While the pundits and the know-it-alls filled the tables and chairs, I preferred to sit at the counter with my back to the madding crowd, supposedly reading the daily paper but actually listening. This was a good idea that didn't work. The store clerks, truck drivers, and farmers at the table would catch sight of me and ask, 'What's your opinion, Mr Q? Should they fire the guy? Was he stealing the city blind? How did he get elected, anyhow?' It was impossible not to get involved, when all I wanted was a cup of coffee and a few minutes' rest after ending my beat or standing in line at the bank and at the office. One day I carried a New York paper instead of the *Moose County Something*. I sat at the counter to read with my back to the noise . . . and no one bothered me! How to explain it? A small-town phenomenon! From then on, whenever I had my nose in the *Times* or the *Journal*, no one interrupted!

Twelve

On Thursday, a handsome middle-aged woman with reddish brown hair, hatless, drove from Lockmaster to Pickax – turning off the highway on to a trail called Marconi between the public library and the theater arts building. It led through a patch of woods and emerged with a breathtaking view!

One came upon the barn suddenly – four stories high, octagonal, constructed of fieldstone and weathered shingles, with two Siamese cats dancing in a small ground-floor window.

Qwilleran went out to meet her.

'Welcome to the barn, Vivian.'

'One question! Why is this little lane named after the Italian inventor of the wireless telegraph?'

'It's named after an owl in the woods that hoots in Morse code . . . Now come in and meet Koko and Yum Yum.'

His guest said, 'They're still talking – at our Lit Club – about the talk you gave on Stephen Miller's book, *Conversation: A History of a Declining Art* . . . Kip thinks you belong in Lockmaster.'

'I appreciate the compliment,' he said.

'May I ask what brought you to Moose County?'

'An inheritance, and when I had the barn converted, I was hooked. I'll show you the interior. It was the last work of a very talented designer. I feel privileged to preserve his work. The acoustics are incredible.'

They went indoors and the guest gasped over the vast spaces, ramps winding around the interior, the views from the balcony levels – all the while followed by the Siamese like hired security guards.

'They like you!' the host said. 'Do you have cats?'

'We have one of Moira's friendly marmalades at the library – the staff named him Reggie – and I have a bossy Siamese at home, called Caesar.'

'How do you two strong-minded individuals get along?'

'Oh, I let him have his way . . . and he lets me have mine.'

While waiting for lunch to be delivered by the caterer, they had aperitifs in the gazebo. On the way she saw the British Silverlight in the foyer. She asked, 'Do you do cross-country biking?'

'No. Do you?'

'Not since my college days. Memorable times! Especially in the British Isles.'

She raved over the gazebo, screened on eight sides. Vivian had heard about Squunk water and wanted to try it. He recommended a drink he had created called 'Moose County Madness' that consisted of Squunk water and cranberry juice.

Qwilleran said, 'I'd like to put something to you, Vivian. There appears to be a big difference between Lockmaster County and Pickax. Would it be appropriate – or even desirable – for the two counties to close the gap with a show of art hats at each venue?'

Qwilleran went on: 'Once upon a time . . . I'm going to sound like a storyteller . . . there was a Moose County potato farmer named Milo Thackeray, who reared motherless twins, Thurston and Thelma. She was a little taller, stronger, bolder than her brother and always looked after him. They were quite different.

'Thurston went to veterinary college in the east, married another doctor, came home, and started an animal hospital in Lockmaster. They had one son. The more flamboyant Thelma went to California and had a successful career with a private dinner club – never married, but kept a protective eye on her younger brother. His son was a problem.

'Eventually, she retired and came back to Moose County to help, if possible, with her difficult nephew. She brought her rare collection of twenty-five art hats, which were to be the subject of a book and a traveling exhibit . . . All the plans were ruined by the nephew, who destroyed not only the family and himself but the collection of art hats. The family scandal left a stain on the good name of Thackeray. Even the hospital changed its name under a new owner.'

Qwilleran paused for her reaction.

'How very sad,' she murmured.

'But that isn't the end of the tale . . . The twenty-five hats were photographed before they were destroyed, and I can show you the prints!'

Then lunch was served, and they turned to the subject of Thelma Thackeray's dinner club. How as hostess Thelma had always worn a hat as she moved through the dining room, chatting with members . . . and how Thelma had always stolen the show with her exotic headgear at Pickax restaurants like the Old Grist Mill, and the Mackintosh Inn.

Qwilleran said, 'What I want to discuss with you is the size of the show. Someone once said that the more art you look at, the less you see. What I propose is two small exhibitions opening simultaneously at the Lockmaster Library and the Pickax gallery. At the end of a certain length of time, the two shows would be reversed, and showgoers would have yet another thrill.'

'You're absolutely right!' she said. 'Our exhibit case will accommodate a dozen photos without crowding, and I imagine that's true of the one in Pickax.'

After lunch the tables were cleared and the photos of the Thackeray art hats were viewed and lavished with praise and amazement.

Vivian said, 'The hats are much more dramatic than the ones we design here in the boondocks! Who was the photographer?'

'John Bushland. Had a studio in the Inglehart house before it was a restaurant. Now he's on the staff of the *Moose County Something*. I helped him take the shots, acting as photographer's flunky. For the exhibits he'll print them on matte stock and mount them on matte board with easel backs.'

119

'What information will be available for the identification cards?'

'Name of hat, artist, and date.'

'I'm weak with excitement!' she said. 'And to think that it happened on Marconi Trail!'

'One question,' he said. 'Thelma not only wore lizardskin shoes, she kept her hats in lizard-print hatboxes, destroyed along with the hats . . .'

'That's part of the hat hobby. We make our own signature hatboxes. Mine are gray pinstripe. If we could find some lizard-print paper, we could make one of Thelma's signature boxes for each exhibit, as an accent.'

Qwilleran was enthusiastic; she was getting into the spirit. He said, 'If you need any help along the way, Pickax has a new coordinator of community activities. She has ideas and enthusiasm – Daisy Babcock. You are on the same wavelength. I'll have her phone you.'

Later, they returned to the barn interior.

'You don't have a piano,' she remarked, as if noting the absence of indoor plumbing.

'No. My mother was an excellent pianist and wanted to give me lessons, but I preferred sandlot baseball. The barn has a fantastic music system and brilliant acoustics. Lately I've acquired some CDs of the Ledfields playing violin and piano, which I'd like you to hear.'

'I wonder how a grand piano would sound in this environment? Frankie, the piano tuner, gives concerts, you know.' Hearing no reaction, she went on, 'My parents are retiring to Florida and liquidating their furnishings, including a Steingraeber & Söhne grand piano made in Bavaria. Perhaps you'd like to take it on trial. There are several spaces that would be suitable—'

'Hold on! Do you realize this barn is in deep freeze five months of the year? But I'm sure the K Fund would buy it for the forthcoming music center. They could have concerts called the Hartman Series featuring talent from both counties!'

That night Qwilleran wrote in his private journal:

There are times when I wish I had taken those piano lessons! I would have left the high-speed stuff to Joe and concentrated on numbers with crashing chords that would frighten the cats and knock the pictures off the walls.

For the next two weeks Qwilleran was busier than he'd ever been. When Mildred Riker asked, 'Have you heard from Polly?' he replied, 'Polly who?'

There were postcards from Paris, of course, but life in

Pickax was challenging in many directions. The Library Hat Show alone had enlisted his attention in several ways: lining up Daisy Babcock, working with Bushy on prints, finding some lizard-print paper to cover a couple of hatboxes . . . and, yes, lining up G. Allen Barter for the K Fund donation of a Steingraeber grand piano to the music center, not to mention finding Frankie a new page turner and driver, giving a talk to the Senior Health Club on private journals, writing a play titled *The Cat Who Got Elected Dogcatcher*. His Qwill Pen column had to come from the 'trash barrel', meaning bits and pieces of this and that that could appear fascinating to his readers. He hardly had time to feed the cats, let alone read to them from the *Wilson Quarterly*.

Meanwhile, those stunning green postcards from Paris were arriving all over town, and recipients were talking about the beautiful river, all those bridges, the Eiffel Tower and the Arc de Triomphe, and especially the stray cats in the cemetery.

People said, 'How come we don't have stray cats in the cemetery?' . . . It was seen as a cultural deficiency, so citizens proposed a committee to promote it. Qwilleran tactfully declined their invitation to champion their cause with Koko as mascot.

Thirteen

Late Thursday afternoon, when Vivian had returned to Lockmaster and her precocious Caesar, Qwilleran felt the satisfaction of a job well done: the launching of a two-county effort and the discovery of yet another librarian with intelligence, vocabulary . . . and cats.

He phoned the *Moose County Something* and was connected with John Bushland in the darkroom.

'I have news!' Qwilleran said. 'We're going ahead with Thelma's hat pix on matte mounts with easel backs . . . Also, we need to cover a couple of hatboxes in the lizard print that Thelma used. Have you seen any lizard-skin print lately?'

'Frankly, I haven't been looking.'

'It's worth doing, even if we have to have an artist simulate it,' Qwilleran said.

'Janice may have some ideas. She may know an artist in California who produces lizard print,' Bushy added.

Qwilleran said, 'If I can give you any menial help to expedite any of these things, I'm available. And don't forget: charge everything to the K Fund.'

Then it was back to the Qwill Pen until the caterwauling began again: it announced a truck coming through the Marconi Woods.

It pulled up at the kitchen door, announced by the cat ballet in the wide window. It was the Linguini truck, and Alfredo jumped out, reaching for a case of Squunk water.

Qwilleran went to meet him. 'Hey, did I order that? I didn't know I ordered any!'

'You didn't. This is a present – from Daisy and me! There's more, too!' Out came a carton of cat snacks and juices.

Fredo said, 'Daisy and I appreciate everything you did to get her out of that hellhole.'

'She and the new job are perfect for each other . . . How

about you and Nick? Did you get roles in the new musical?'

'Yes, we're doing Mungojerrie and Rumpelteazer. Any time you want to come and sing with us, you're welcome at rehearsal. Have you done any singing? Your voice sounds like it.'

'Only in college, but I enjoyed it! Is the pianist back on the job?'

'Frankie? Yeah, that was a crime what happened to little Libby!' Fredo gave his listener a swift glance. 'And I really mean *crime*!' He jumped into the cab. 'Thanks again from Daisy and me.'

'One question,' Qwilleran said. 'What is the arrangement you have with Frankie? I understand he doesn't drive.'

'We take turns picking him up . . . Wanna volunteer?' Fredo added in a jocular afterthought.

'I might do just that!' said Qwilleran. 'I have a lot of space to fill in the Qwill Pen, and I might find a story on piano tuning. Why does a grown man – with an assortment of talents – get called *Frankie*?'

'His dad is Franklin, and they're sort of an old-fashioned family.'

Fredo gunned the motor – and scatted the cats away from the window.

The conversation had reminded Qwilleran of all the half sentences and innuendos he had heard at Lois's Luncheonette.

The Siamese were waiting for him near their feeding station. He asked, 'What really happened to Libby Simms?'

They looked at each other and then jumped off the counter, and chased up and down the ramp.

Finishing his thousand words, the newsman took his New York paper and went to Lois's Luncheonette for some scuttlebutt.

Before he could take the end seat at the counter and open his paper, Lois lumbered up. With all due respect to the heavyset proprietress, that was how she moved about her premises – slowly and with grandeur. The columnist was one of her favorite customers; she served him not only coffee but a slice of chocolate cake and some turkey scraps for the cats on the house.

He opened his newspaper and tuned in to the babble behind him:

'The city's hired someone to keep a check on all the goings-on.'
'No kiddin'! Who?'

'Fredo Linguini's wife.'

'She's a lively one.'

'They're giving her an office in the old community hall building.'

'I hope they fix it up for her. It's showing its age.'

'Aren't we all? All it needs is some paint. If they called for volunteers, I'd sign up! We're lucky to have that building. We had our wedding reception there.'

During Polly's absence, Qwilleran had plenty of dinner invitations, and one evening he was dining with the Bushlands. They discussed the forthcoming exhibit of Bushy's hat photos. Janice, who had been Thelma's assistant for years, was now assisting Bushy in the photographer's darkroom.

Qwilleran asked, 'Do you remember Thelma's lizard-print hatboxes?'

'Yes, she had them custom-made. There's still some lizard-print paper in her closet.'

'What!' Qwilleran almost dropped a forkful of sweet-potato pie.

After that, everything happened fast. A motorcycle messenger was summoned, and two rolls of the unusual paper were dispatched to Lockmaster.

By the time he returned to the barn, there was a

message from Vivian on the phone: 'A miracle! How did you do it?'

He called Vivian back and said, 'Abracadabra! An old sideshow trick!'

'And Daisy Babcock is going to meet with me,' she said. 'On the phone she sounds charming!'

The venerable community hall was part of the City of Stone in downtown Pickax. Several generations had trooped in and out of its doors for meetings, lectures, parties, business luncheons, exhibits, cat and dog shows, and antique auctions. Several generations of janitors had shuffled chairs, tables, platforms, and runways accordingly. Although the rooms were plain – clean but plain – it occurred to Qwilleran that Daisy's presence would inspire changes: a little paint, some art on the walls, even background music.

It gave Qwilleran an idea!

The forthcoming publication of the Homer Tibbitt biography would no doubt be introduced by a program at the community hall. Homer had been born in Moose County, had attended college in Lockmaster County, and had been principal of Central High School there until his retirement.

Homer then returned to his home territory and served as honorary Moose County historian until his death at the age of a hundred. During that time he wrote hundreds of research papers now on file in the public library, and his feisty sense of humor made the citizens laugh.

Qwilleran's idea – to mark the publication of the grand Old Man's biography – was to rename the community hall the Homer Tibbitt Auditorium.

He proceeded circumspectly – pulled strings – and hinted at K Fund backing.

That evening, as Qwilleran gave the cats their bedtime treat, he mused at the changes awaiting Polly's return: the two-county show of art hats . . . the Homer Tibbitt Auditorium . . . Vivian's offer of a grand piano . . . the young girl's death from a bee sting – just like that of Maggie Sprenkle's husband.

Koko interrupted with a loud 'Yow-w-w!' as if saying, 'Let's go! Let's go!'

The next morning, Qwilleran drove downtown to the department store. He and Larry looked at Polly's postcard of the Champs Elysées. Qwilleran told the joke about the tourist who thought she was a Parisienne in her Lanspeak's raincoat. Qwilleran bought an alligator belt for himself. He had always wanted one, but Polly didn't like them.

So far, so good, he told himself. And then he had a

phone call from Steve Bestover in Lockmaster . . . the attorney who was Shirley's son.

'Mr Qwilleran. I hope I'm not calling too early.' It sounded urgent.

'Not at all. It sounds important.'

'The girls have been in an accident. It could be worse, but they're hospitalized, and it changes their plans. They were due to fly home this weekend.'

'What happened?'

'They were in a taxi that was hit by a car exceeding the speed limit. Polly has a few bumps and cuts, but Mother has a neck injury that causes back pain. She says they're getting the best of care and not to worry, but they can't leave as planned. I will fly over when I get the signal and accompany them home.'

'Do you have a number I can call?'

'Polly says it will be better if she calls you. She'll phone collect when she has some information. The odd thing is that it happened in the Pont de l'Alma tunnel, where Princess Diana was killed.'

'Yow!' came a blast in Qwilleran's free ear.

'Was that your Koko?'

'He knows bad news when he hears it. Thanks for calling, Steve. Sorry we've never met. Keep in touch.'

Then Qwilleran regarded the cat strangely. He had been

jumping on and off the desk. It was only when he heard about the tunnel accident that he responded – did he know that was where Princess Diana was killed . . . or what?

Fourteen

In most communities, half the citizens like a change once in a while; the other half likes everything the way it is. It was no different 400 miles north of everywhere. The proposed beautification of the community hall was considered either a calamity or a delight. The town's leading designer was offering her expertise. Without charge. She was the daughter of Andrew Brodie, Pickax police chief, and Qwilleran found it an excuse to invite his chum to the barn for a nightcap.

Qwilleran refrained from using the the old cliché 'Long time no see', but the first words the chief said were 'Long time no see.'

Andy took a seat at the bar, and his host reached for the Scotch bottle. 'The usual?'

'Still drinking that stuff?' the chief said in disdain as Qwilleran poured Squunk water for himself.

'What do you hear about the new community hall, Andy?' Qwilleran asked, although he knew the answer.

'I hear they're changing the name. Keeping it secret. I hear they're using wallpaper and fancy things like that.'

'Whatever your daughter suggests will be in good taste,' Qwilleran ventured. 'It's generous of the stores to donate the paint – and some of our foremost loafers to donate their labor . . . What are you buying your wife for Christmas, Andy?'

Daisy Babcock, the new county coordinator, had been busy coordinating the details of the event: the building itself had a face-lift. Qwilleran would preview his new biography of Homer Tibbitt. Rhoda, his widow, would come in from Ittibittiwassee Estates with two busloads of her neighbors and would be presented with flowers. A baritone from their church choir would sing 'He's a Grand Old Man' to the tune of 'It's a Grand Old Flag'. Longtime friends would tell amusing tales from Homer's later years, including the Brown Paper Bag Mystery. A delegation of notables would christen the old hall the Homer Tibbitt Auditorium. It would be filmed.

Daisy Babcock, working with Fran Brodie, had planned a decorative scheme based on the Pickax High School colors: gray, black, and gold. The building was gray stone; the athletic team was the Gray Panthers. Rhoda Tibbitt's flowers were yellow roses. The commemorative programs with Homer's photo on the cover were also yellow.

The weatherbeaten sign across the top of the entrance had been replaced with HOMER TIBBITT AUDITORIUM in crisp black letters touched with gold. And the shabby wooden doors in the wide entrance were now shiny black with brass hardware.

Qwilleran had interviewed countless citizens in writing the biography and planning the celebration, but nowhere did he reveal the secret of the Brown Paper Bag!

In his private journal that night, Qwilleran reported:

Homer came from a family of teetotalers and throughout his life he was never known to take a drink, but he delighted in teasing folks. In his adult life and well into his nineties, he carried a brown paper bag in his pocket, and it contained a flask of amber liquid from which he was known to take a swig occasionally. Even his closest friends were never allowed to share the secret. When, at the age of ninety, he finally married, it was expected that Rhoda would track down the truth. She never did. He managed to keep his secret to the end. He had a great sense of humor and kept on laughing at folks.

During Polly's absence, Qwilleran received many invitations to dinner. One of them was from Lyle and Lisa Compton in their condo. For a fourth they invited a neighbor, Barbara Honiger. He knew the name. She contributed regularly to the Qwill Pen column and boasted to the Comptons that she had received enough yellow pencils from the Qwill Pen to build the foundation of a log cabin.

Barbara was not tall but had a commanding personality and sharp wit – an attorney with her own practice, specializing in real estate.

She had good-natured opinions on everything. A meal at the Comptons' was always a lively talkfest, even though Lisa made no claims to cooking skills. No one asked any questions about the casserole she served, although it tasted pretty good, and conversation never lagged.

LYLE: 'I like your alligator belt, Qwill. Lisa won't let me have one.'

QWILL: 'Polly dislikes them, too, so as soon as she left the country, I splurged.'

LISA: 'When are you closing the barn?'

BARBARA: 'How do you go about closing a barn?'

QWILL: 'Pat O'Dell and his crew swarm all over the place.'

LYLE: 'Better do it before we have zero temperature and four feet of snow!'

QWILL: 'I was waiting until after the Lit Club meeting. I'm putting up the speaker overnight.'

LISA: 'That's changed. There's been a death in his family. Could you speak to the Lit Club, Qwill?'

After a thoughtful pause for dramatic effect, he said, 'What would you think of forming a secret society named Word Tasters Anonymous? . . . Anyone can join . . . no dues!' There was a stunned silence, and he went on. 'It's a theory currently being tested. Words have flavor as well as meaning. Words can be enjoyed on many levels. Dickens is a master of the art. Consider the last lines in *A Tale of Two Cities*.'

He quoted: ' "It is a far, far better thing that I do, than I have ever done; it is a far, far better rest that I go to than I have ever known." '

Following nods and murmurs from his listeners, he went on:

'When I say those words, I can taste their exquisite sweetness . . . In *A Christmas Carol* I feel the crispy crunchiness of consonants, vowels, and diphthongs, delighting my taste buds.' He quoted: ' "Then up rose Mrs Cratchit, Cratchit's wife, dressed out but poorly in a twice-turned gown, but brave in ribbons, which are cheap and make a goodly show for sixpence." '

He explained, 'Everyone knows there are music lovers, but few know that there are word lovers too: aware of the taste and feeling and magic of words, not necessarily the meanings. One of our members is a successful business-woman who loved four words from Shakespeare: "Nothing comes from nothing." The arrangement of friendly consonants reassured her.'

Qwilleran said, 'Word tasting is not limited to the work of great writers. Mildred Riker gets a shiver of pleasure from a practice sentence used in high school when learning to type.'

Everyone wanted to know it, and he quoted: ' "The time of many murders is after midnight." '

Then, Barbara asked, 'I suppose you've all seen Thelma's hat photos at the bookstore?'

LYLE: 'I hear the locals like the new showcases better than the hats.'

QWILL: 'The hats were designed by California artists.

Their taste is a little sophisticated for Moose County. I had to gulp myself at some of their productions, but I hear the library-goers in Lockmaster are so excited they can hardly wait to see the other half of the show; they're coming up here to the bookstore to see it.'

Qwilleran enjoyed meeting Barbara. He liked attorneys. He looked forward to meeting Steve Bestover. He enjoyed his K Fund sessions with G. Allen Barter, who was less of a legal eagle and more of a brother-in-law.

On Mrs Fulgrove's last two visits to clean the barn . . . or 'fluff it up', as she said, she and her housecleaners covered the premises, frightening the cats . . . and then she always left a note. Qwilleran saved them for what he called the Fulgrove Witchery Collection. Her syntax was curious, to say the least.

Dear Mr Q . . . Koko broke a bottle on your bathroom floor which I saved the pieces of glass so you could see what it was.

It proved to be Scottish aftershave lotion from Canada that Polly had brought from one of her trips. The following week, a porcelain figurine of a bagpiper in shoulder plaid, kilt, and knee hose was found on the living-room hearth in several fragments.

Dear Mr Q . . . I think Koko did it . . . which he was hanging around, looking naughty. I told him he was a bad cat which he ran away. He never broke anything before . . .

Yours truly . . . Mrs Fulgrove

Just as Qwilleran was beginning to suspect Koko of anti-Scottish tendencies, all of a sudden he witnessed a third misdemeanor. He saw Koko tear the cover of a book Polly had given him. It was only a paperback, but it was twentieth-century poems that they both enjoyed.

He thought, That cat is trying to tell me something. Does he think she should not have left Brutus and Catta with strangers? Who knows what enters his feline mind? The cats are probably eating better at Pet Plaza than they ever did at home.

Fifteen

And then Polly dropped a bombshell!

Dearest Qwill,
I have thrilling news, and I know you'll be excited for
me. Steven has come over to escort Shirley home, and
I'm staying here for a while!

An American firm with offices in Paris advertised
for a librarian to handle their commercial library,
which is extensive.

I applied and was given a three-year contract!
Can you believe it? It's technical, but I'm a fast

learner. I simply can't believe my good fortune!

I'm notifying Dr Connie to find a good home for Brutus and Catta, preferably together. And I'm asking Mildred to conduct a house sale and sell everything of mine to benefit the church. It's not very good stuff, having belonged to my in-laws for ages before I got it. I can buy all new things when I return.

I'll miss dining out with you and the musicals at the barn.

Love,
Polly

Qwilleran phoned Dr Connie to inquire about Brutus and Catta and learned they were living it up at the Pet Plaza and might never want to leave.

He read Polly's letter again to see if he had misunderstood. It was perfectly clear. He told himself he had been the recipient of a 'Dear John' letter for the first time in his life . . . Perhaps he had been too complacent . . . they had been 'together', so to speak, for a long time!

The Siamese hovered around. They knew something was wrong.

It soon appeared that Polly had notified everyone. Always businesslike and thorough, she had sent news releases to the *Something* and *Ledger*, resulting in front-page coverage. The headlines also started the gossip mills grinding.

At Toodle's Market: Did you know she spoke French? . . . She went to college Down East. Her family's not from around here . . . Her father was a professor . . . She married a student from Moose County; that's how she landed here.

At the drugstore: Did you know she was a widow from way back? Her husband was a volunteer fireman killed while fighting a barn fire . . . Wonder why she never remarried . . . She went to work in the Pickax library; that's what she was trained for. But she never remarried.

At Lois's Luncheonette: Looks like his girlfriend ran out on him . . . He won't have any trouble getting a replacement.

At the post office: She went to our church. He never came with her, but he was a generous giver . . . No wonder! With all that money he has to pay tax on! . . . I'd gladly pay the tax if I had all that dough!

And now everyone was phoning Qwilleran . . . neighbors at the condo . . . bookstore crew . . . Polly's hairdresser . . . No one knew that she was fluent in French. People thought that the French magazine that was always on her coffee table was only stage dressing, so to speak.

Qwilleran hurried to the bookstore and had a conference with Judd Amhurst; no problem there, other than shock . . .

The Rikers invited him to dinner – alone – and he declined, saying he had a deadline in connection with his next book . . .

In the days that followed, Qwilleran, who had once trained for the stage, acted as if nothing had happened.

Still, at eleven P.M., he found himself thinking: Let's face it. Everyone needs a late-night phone pal.

'. . . What are you doing? Did you have a good day? . . . What did the vet say about Catta's stomach upset? . . . Where would you like to have dinner Saturday night? . . . I finished reading my book. I wouldn't recommend it. Well, let me know about the plumber's decision . . . *À bientôt.*'

Then Qwilleran pulled a few strings.

Polly's unit at the Willows was up for lease; Barbara Honiger had mentioned that it would be nice living closer to town. Both Joe Bunker and Dr Connie thought an attorney would be an asset to the Willows.

Qwilleran looked up a phone number.

'Good evening, Barbara,' he said in his mellifluous voice. 'I hear you're moving into the Willows! We couldn't hope for a better addition. Is there anything I can do to expedite your move?'

The Willows celebrated the arrival of Barbara Honiger's cat, Molasses, with . . . not another pizza party but . . . a catered meal by the Mackintosh Inn, delivered by a busboy in a chef's tall toque.

Toasts were drunk to the new neighbor. She showed snapshots of Molasses, her marmalade. They were a congenial group. Joe Bunker played 'Kitten on the Keys' very fast. He said he had just had his piano tuned. Barbara was impressed by Joe's high-speed performance at the piano. Dr Connie gave the newcomer a token gift from Scotland, a Shetland-wool scarf. Qwilleran invited them to a performance of the musical *Cats*.

With a commanding stance and a grand gesture, Qwilleran declared, 'I consider it significant that Shakespeare made no mention of newspaper columnists in his vast work . . . or of veterinarians or meteorologists. But he mentions attorneys!'

There were cries of 'Who? Where? Which play?'

'In act two of *Henry VI, Part II* . . . "First thing we do . . . we kill all the lawyers"!'

The festivities lasted longer than the usual pizza party; the hotel had sent over four courses. Dr Connie showed the movie of her trip to Scotland. Joe's piano playing seemed particularly brilliant.

Barbara asked Qwilleran, 'Is that portrait of Lady

Mackintosh in the hotel lobby your mother?'

'Yes. Amazingly, it was done by a local artist who'd never met her or seen her photo. He was merely told she resembled Greer Garson. Yet the portrait doesn't look like a movie star; she looks like my mother.'

Joe said, 'I should have him do a portrait of my father – a horseradish farmer with a moustache and glasses. He looked like Teddy Roosevelt.'

Qwilleran accompanied the women to their units and went in to say hello to the new cat on the block.

Barbara owned one of Moira MacDiarmid's cats. 'Or he owns me. He's in the deepest tawny tone like a molasses cookie, so I named him Molasses, and he seems to like it.'

Qwilleran noted that his markings, tilted over one eye, gave him the jaunty look of a soldier.

He sang an old military tune: 'There's something about Molasses, there's something about Molasses, there's something about Molasses that is fine, fine, fine.'

Molasses fell over sideways – an expression of approval, Barbara said.

When he returned to the barn, the Siamese greeted him with that reproachful stare that meant their bedtime snack was late.

* * *

That evening, instead of waiting for the call that never came, Qwilleran made one of his own – to Wetherby Goode. 'Joe. Great party! Great music!'

'Yeah, you can always tell when old Betsey has been tuned. I pound the ivories so hard, she has to be tuned four times a year. It has something to do with the felts and the hammers. Don't ask me what!'

'Really? Who does it?'

'Young guy in Lockmaster.'

Qwilleran asked, 'Would Dr Feltzanhammer make a good story for the Qwill Pen?'

'I don't know. He's young and kind of shy. But he's likable.'

'I'll give it a try. Before interviewing anyone on an esoteric subject, I read all about it in the encyclopedia, so I know what questions to ask and what he's talking about. What are felts and hammers? My mother was a brilliant pianist, and she never mentioned felts and hammers.'

'By the way, it was the piano tuner's girlfriend who was killed by a bee sting at the Old Manse.'

At that moment, Koko interrupted with a gut-wrenching howl.

'What was that all about?' Joe asked.

'Koko wants the lights turned out.'

Qwilleran knew better. It was the cat's death howl. It meant wrongful death.

Sixteen

In spite of the ups and downs of his current life, Qwilleran had the steadying influence of home and workplace: feeding the cats twice a day and writing the Qwill Pen twice a week. Filling the thousand-word hole on page two kept him alert for ideas.

The morning after Joe's party, Qwilleran was feeding the cats when he received an unexpected phone call from Rhoda Tibbitt.

'Qwill, I hope I'm not calling too early. I have exciting news. I've discovered the answer to the Brown Paper Bag Mystery! I was preparing Homer's suits to give to charity, the way he wanted, and I found some little brown paper bags in the pockets! And two of them contained tiny flasks.' She paused for breath – or effect. 'I tasted the contents: one of them still had . . . black breakfast tea! And the other had the afternoon tea that Homer liked. Lapsang souchong!'

Qwilleran said, 'Don't say a word to anyone! They're talking about a refreshment stand for the lobby of the auditorium, something with class . . . and I'm going to suggest the Homer Tibbitt Tearoom! . . . But don't explain, and neither will I. We'll keep Homer's secret.'

Qwilleran had an opportunity to use his privileged information from Rhoda Tibbitt when he called on Daisy Babcock in the refurbished auditorium. He complimented her on the metamorphosis of the building, and she praised his book review. There were daisies from Fredo on her desk – and a daisy wallpaper on the wall above a gray dado.

She said, 'We've been thinking about a refreshment stand on the main floor – not a hangout for kids but something more civilized.'

'How about a Homer Tibbitt Tearoom?'

'Qwill. You come up with the best impromptu ideas!'

A chart on the wall gave the status of local projects. The Old Manse Museum of Art and Antiques was open two days a week with trained guides – twenty dollars a ticket – and people coming from all over the country – even Europe. She then added, 'But they won't go into the garden. They've all heard about the danger of bee stings.'

'Have you had any more trouble?' he asked.

She shook her head and looked sad.

Also on the chart were the following:

Senior Health Club – Ready next year.

Wildlife museum – Buildings
finished/mounted animals and art
being moved in.

There was a photo of the Ledfields on Daisy's desk, and Qwilleran said, 'Handsome couple. I never met them, but their efforts for child welfare alone were commendable.'

Daisy said, 'That's because they were childless and regretful. Bringing busloads of kids from Pickax Schools to view the mounted animals gave Nathan great pleasure. He would be thrilled to know that we're erecting two buildings downtown and the city is renaming the Old Back Road the Ledfield Highway.'

Cats musical – Now being rehearsed.

Qwilleran asked, 'How are the *Cats* rehearsals progressing? Is Frankie still the accompanist? Who's turning Frankie's pages?'

'Uncle Louie's wife. Hannah. She's a wonderful woman and does what needs to be done. She can accompany the chorus or even direct the show, and yet she'll sweep the stage if necessary, or make sandwiches for the cast. It's amazing what the McLeods have done with the orphan they adopted.'

'So is Frankie doing all right?'

'It appears so.'

He asked, 'Do you think he would make a good interview on piano tuning? I could kill a couple of birds with one stone and do chauffeur service for a rehearsal.'

'I know. This is what we've worked out. We could drop off Frankie at the barn, and you could drive him back to the theater at seven-thirty. You could give him a bite to eat; he isn't fussy, and he'd love to see the barn and meet the cats. I know the barn doesn't have a piano, but Frankie has one of those roll-up keyboards!'

Qwilleran agreed. 'You're an expert coordinator, Daisy.'

He had decided against doing a Qwill Pen column on piano tuning. It was another no-story.

When one of the Linguini brothers (Mungojerrie, not Rumpelteazer) arrived at the barn, Frankie jumped out the passenger side, gazing in rapture at the lofty barn and saying, 'Oh, wow! Oh, wow!'

Qwilleran realized high praise when he heard it.

Koko and Yum Yum were cavorting in the kitchen window as they always did when a vehicle arrived, and – as first-time visitors always did – Frankie asked, 'Are these your cats?'

Qwilleran always felt like saying, 'No, these are a pair of pet crocodiles.' But he said amiably, 'Yes, this is Koko and Yum Yum.'

Both Qwilleran and the Siamese found Frankie a likable guest. The Siamese followed him around and put on their flying-squirrel act from the top balcony to entertain him.

The Siamese were fascinated by the 'thing' strapped to his back, somewhat like a blanket roll but actually a four-octave electronic piano. (Later, when they heard it, though, they went and hid.)

'Do you come from a musical family?' Qwilleran asked.

'My dad raises horses, but my mother is a piano teacher, and I have an uncle who's a piano tuner.'

'Did he teach you about felts and hammers?' He was enjoying a private joke.

'He taught me everything,' Frankie said seriously.

That explained everything except his inability to drive,

and his friendship with Libby Simms had taken care of that.

Locals in both counties had said, 'They're a darling couple. Do you think they'll marry? It's a touching romance.' And then there was the incident of the bee sting.

Now Qwilleran was about to show Frankie the premises.

'First we must order our dinner,' Qwilleran said, handing his guest a menu card. 'Order anything you like and it'll be delivered in fifteen minutes. I'm having ham and sweet potatoes with asparagus spears . . . a cheese muffin . . . apple-and-walnut salad . . . and chocolate cake. I have my own coffee machine.'

'I'll have the same,' Frankie said.

'While we're waiting, Koko will show you their apartment on the third level. They have a twistletwig rocking chair that you might try sitting in; it's an experience.'

Apparently the three of them were 'communicating', because Frankie had to be called down for dinner. It was served in the screened gazebo, and that was another experience, since small animals came up to the screen and communed silently with the Siamese.

Frankie said, 'Libby would have loved this. Did you ever meet her?'

'Yes. Charming young woman.'

Two tears rolled down the young man's face. 'Now my

life's ruined. Libby and I . . . we were gonna get married and travel around on concert tours. But she went out to the garden without the kit the doctor gave her.'

'I hear she kept it in the pocket of her garden coat.'

'Yeah, but she wore that jacket when we went on dates, too. She must've taken the bee kit out and forgot to put it back. She ruined my life as well as her own.'

The Siamese, not used to seeing anyone cry, came forward to watch, and stroking them gave Frankie some comfort.

From then on, he was a sullen guest . . . 'I hafta get back to the theater.' He jumped up and bolted out to Qwilleran's vehicle without a word to the cats.

Qwilleran drove him back to the concert hall. He dropped him without receiving thanks, but Daisy was in the lobby.

'Thanks, Qwill! How did it go?'

'Okay, but I think he was nervous about getting back on time.'

After dropping off Frankie unceremoniously at the concert hall, Qwilleran returned to the barn to feed the cats and was greeted by two agitated Siamese. It meant the phone had been ringing but no message had been left.

He prepared their plate of food and watched them devour it, but they did so nervously, with frequent glances toward the back door. While they were bent over their plates the phone rang – and they jumped a foot.

Daisy was calling from the theater. 'Frankie got back on time but he was a wreck. Hannah had to sub for him. What happened?'

Qwilleran said, 'Bears discussing, but not over the phone. I'll see you tomorrow.'

Writing in his journal that night, he remembered overhearing conversations in the coffee shop after the girl died from a bee sting at the Old Manse. One always heard gossips sounding off. They had been saying: Sounds fishy to me! . . . They're not telling the whole ball of wax . . . My cousin works at the Old Manse, and she says they're not allowed to talk about the accident.

As the press had been led to believe, it would affect public response to the Old Manse and its gardens. And it had.

Seventeen

Late Saturday night, Qwilleran phoned Wetherby Goode at the Willows.

'Joe, I'm tired of living in the Taj Mahal of Pickax and showing it off to every visiting celebrity. We're moving back to the Willows.'

'Good! We'll have a pizza party!'

'Will you bring Connie and Barbara down here for Sunday supper and a concert? As you know, the acoustics are incredible, and I have some recordings of the Ledfields' violin-and-piano duets that I have to return to Maggie Sprenkle. Pat O'Dell will deliver the food. Then we'll all go up to the Willows and be ready for the *Cats* show next Saturday.'

On Sunday afternoon the delegation from the Willows arrived at the barn bearing gifts: Wetherby: a bottle of something; Connie: homemade cookies; Barbara: a tape recording of a jazz combo.

The two women, first-time visitors, were escorted up the ramp by the Siamese to enjoy the fabulous view.

Qwilleran said, 'Try sitting in their twistletwig rocker for a stimulating experience.'

It apparently worked, because all four were frisky when they returned to the main floor.

Qwilleran thought, Well, anyway, it's the last time I'll have to go through this charade for six months.

They consulted the caterer's menu, orders were placed, and they had aperitifs around the big square coffee table while waiting for the delivery, during which Koko returned to the top balcony and did his flying-squirrel act, landing on a sofa cushion between the two women guests. They screamed; drinks were spilled. Qwilleran said, 'Bad cat!' The two men made an effort to keep a straight face.

There was plenty of conversation about Connie's spring trip to Scotland and Barbara's annual visit to the Shakespeare Festival in Canada. Wetherby said he never went anywhere but Horseradish.

Dinners were delivered. The decision was made to serve in the gazebo, where it was cool but pleasant.

Connie said, 'The residents of Indian Village are agitating to have the open decks screened for summer, if it can be done without darkening the interiors. When are you moving back, Qwill?'

'Tomorrow!' he promised.

Then questions were asked about the barn: Who designed the remodeling? Is there a lot of upkeep? Are you handy with tools?

Qwilleran said, 'You probably know Ben Kosley. He takes care of emergencies. I wrote a poem of praise about him in my column. Would you like to hear it? It sums up life in an old apple barn.' He read it to them.

Call 911-BEN-K
The locks don't lock; the floorboards squeak;
The brand new washer has sprung a leak!
The phone needs moving; the pipes have burst!
You're beginning to think the barn is cursed!
CALL Ben!
There's a hole in the floor; the windows stick.
You need some help with the toilet – quick!
The chandelier is out of plumb.
The electric outlets are starting to HUM!

DON'T WORRY . . . CALL Ben!
The sliding door could use a new lock;
There's something wrong with the oven clock.
The garbage disposal refuses to grind.
The dryer won't dry. You're losing your mind!
NO PROBLEM . . . CALL Ben!
The TV cable is on the wrong wall.
The bedroom ceiling is threatening to fall.
There's a great big crack in a windowpane.
A wristwatch fell down the bathroom drain!
OOPS! . . . CALL Ben!
The porch roof is hanging from two or three nails!
When anyone sneezes, the power fails!
A buzzer just buzzed . . .
A bell just rang . . .
THE KITCHEN BLEW UP WITH A TERRIBLE BANG!
DON'T PANIC! . . . CALL Ben!

Then they asked about the history of the barn – if any happened to be known.

'Yes – if you're not squeamish. It's something I've never talked about.'

He had their rapt attention.

'The property dates back to the days of strip farms, two hundred feet wide and a mile long. What is now the back

160

road was then the front yard and the location of the farmhouse. Apples were the crop, and this was the apple barn. We knew the name of the family, but we didn't know what had become of them, and we don't know why the farmer hanged himself from the barn rafters.'

Qwilleran's listeners looked around as if searching for a clue.

'The family moved away, and the property was abandoned until an enterprising realtor sold it to the Klingenschoen Foundation. I needed a place to live, and the K Fund had money to invest in the town. We hired an architectural designer from Down Below, who is responsible for the spectacular interior. And we don't know why he, too, hanged himself from the rafters.'

There was a long pause. Then Barbara jumped up and said she had to go home and feed Molasses. Connie jumped up, too, and said she had to go home and feed Bonnie Lassie.

'Wonderful party!' they both said.

'Let's do it again!' Wetherby said, and the party ended without the playing of the Ledfield recordings.

The pocket-size gift that Barbara had brought Qwilleran from Canada temporarily disappeared during the move to the Willows – but reappeared appropriately in a pocket of his coat. It was a tape recording of a jazz combo with swaggering syncopation that churned his blood and revived memories. The Siamese also reacted favorably. Their ears twitched, they sprang at each other, grappled, kicked, and otherwise had a good time.

When Qwilleran checked in at the bookstore that week, Judd Amhurst sermonized on the Literary Club problem: 'The time has come for forgetting about lecturers from Down Below who have to be paid and then cancel at the last minute. We can stage our own programs!'

'Good! Never liked Proust anyway! What do you have in mind?'

'More member participation? Remember how Homer Tibbitt liked *Lasca*? Lyle Compton likes "The Highwayman" by Alfred Noyes, early twentieth century.'

'Favorite of mine, too. He was an athlete, and there's an athletic vigor in his poetry.'

'Lyle says there's a cops-and-robbers flavor to the story.'

'And the poet has a forceful way of repeating words.'

Qwilleran quoted: ' "He rode with a jeweled twinkle . . . His pistol butts a-twinkle . . . His rapier hilt a-twinkle, under the jeweled sky." '

Dundee came running and wrapped himself around Qwilleran's ankle.

* * *

In Pickax, Qwilleran's annual move from barn to condo was as well known as the Fourth of July parade. The printers ran off a hundred announcements, and students addressed the envelopes. Mrs McBee made a winter supply of chocolate chip cookies. Friends, neighbors, fellow newsmen, and business associates were properly notified. And on moving day, the Siamese went and hid.

Nevertheless, the move was always successfully accomplished, and Qwilleran's household was relocated for another six months.

Eighteen

That night Qwilleran wrote in his private journal:

It's good to get back to the country quiet of the condo. I had Chief Brodie in for a nightcap before leaving, and he said he would keep an eye on the barn. I returned the Ledfield recording to Maggie Sprenkle and had my last nice cup of tea for a while. I've decided 'nice' is a euphemism for 'weak', bless her soul.

And there was a message from Daisy Babcock on the

machine: 'Qwill, sorry to bother you but I've discovered a disturbing situation at the office, and Fredo said I should ask you to look at it. I don't want to talk about it on the phone.'

Nineteen

Unanswered questions always made Qwilleran nervous, and he slept poorly after receiving Daisy's message. The Siamese slept very well. After living in the round for six months, they gladly adjusted to the straight walls and square corners of the condo. The units were open plan, with bedrooms off the balcony and a two-story wall of glass overlooking the open deck and the creek. In front of the fireplace, two cushiony sofas faced each other across a large cocktail table on a deep shag rug. It would make a good landing pad for an airborne Siamese, dropping in from the balcony railing.

Qwilleran told them to be good, and their innocent expressions convinced him that a naughty impulse never entered their sleek heads.

The distance to downtown Pickax was longer than that from the barn, and so Qwilleran drove, parking behind the auditorium. Walking around to the front of the building, he bowed and saluted to greetings and the usual question: 'How's Koko, Mr Q?'

When he arrived at Daisy's office upstairs, the hallway was piled with empty cartons waiting for the trash collection. Her door was open. There were more boxes inside. Daisy was on the phone. She waved him in and pointed to a chair. She was speaking to her husband.

'Fredo, Qwill has arrived, so I'll talk to you later.'

Qwilleran was reminded of the Box Bank at the Old Manse: cartons, clothing boxes, hatboxes, and shoe boxes.

Daisy's greeting was 'Excuse the mess. Throw something off a chair seat and sit down.' She jumped up and closed the door to the hallway.

'I see you finally moved out,' he said lamely. 'It looks as if you raided the Box Bank.'

'I had accumulated so many things – clothing for all seasons, beautiful books that the Ledfields had given me, magazines we subscribed to and couldn't bear to throw away, and desk drawers full of pens, pencils, cosmetics, all kinds of personal items. The women at the Manse brought me boxes, and I just dumped things in them. It was Alma's day off, and I wanted to get out to avoid a scene.'

'I can understand,' he murmured.

She handed him a shoe box. 'Open this and tell me what you see. Don't touch.'

He did as told, and asked, 'Is it toothpaste?' The fat tube was lying facedown, showing only fine print on the back.

'It's the missing bee kit! No one else in the Manse had ever had one. Someone must have sneaked it from Libby's jacket and tossed it into the Box Bank, perhaps expecting to retrieve it later and blame Libby for carelessness. Who knows? Fredo said you'd know what to do.'

'Hand me the phone,' Qwilleran said. 'We'll get George Barter here to look at it. Fingerprints might be the answer.'

He declined coffee and said he wanted to think for a few minutes. Daisy left him alone, and he remembered what he'd heard.

Libby suspected that Nathan's treasures, being sold for child welfare, were not reaching their intended charity. She wanted to accuse Alma to her face but had been advised not to be hasty. Libby had apparently made the mistake of impetuous youth. She was defending her Uncle Nathan's wishes, and his memory.

The law office was only a block away, and Barter arrived as Qwilleran was leaving. They saluted and shook their heads in disbelief. Arch Riker had been right: 'When there's so much money floating around, somebody's going to get greedy.'

Qwilleran went to his parked car to think. Koko was always right – no matter what! The cat had sensed something wrong at the moment of Libby's death. His gut-wrenching death howl was never mistaken. It meant that someone, somewhere, was the victim of murder. In fact, there were times when Koko sensed it was going to happen before the fact! When Alma visited the barn, Koko tried to frighten her. He tore up her black-and-gold catalog. He staged a scene over the used books that came in a box that originally held a punch bowl sold by Alma. He made a fuss over the pocket-size copy of *The Portrait of a Lady*. Was it because the author was Henry *James*? Not likely, Qwilleran thought, but who knows? And then there was Koko's reaction to Polly's accident in Paris – at the Pont de l'Alma tunnel.

Qwilleran hoped he would never be asked to state all of this on the witness stand. 'They'd put me away,' he said aloud. And yet . . .

He drove to Lois's Luncheonette with his New York paper to listen to gossip. Everywhere, there were pedestrians in twos and threes, talking about the scandal; one could tell by their grave expressions.

At Lois's, the tables were filled. He sat at the counter, ordered coffee and a roll, and buried his head in his paper. From the tables came snatches of comments like:

'Nothing like this ever happened here!'

'They bring people in from Lockmaster, that's what's wrong.'

'Nothing's been proved, but everyone knows.'

'Imagine! It happened in a city museum!'

'Nathan will be turnin' over in his grave!'

'My daughter-in-law says she has a friend . . .'

Everyone was talking about the Purple Point Scandal, preferring to associate it with the affluent suburb rather than nature's useful honeybee. Qwilleran returned home to the Willows and avoided answering the inevitable phone calls. They could be screened by the answering device.

One was from Wetherby Goode: 'Qwill, looking forward to the *Cats* show Saturday night. I'll provide the transportation. The gals will provide the supper. Barbara wants to know if cat food will be appropriate.'

Qwilleran liked Barbara's sense of humor. When invited in to meet Molasses, he liked her taste in design, too.

171

Replacing Polly's elderly heirlooms was a roomful of blond modern furniture, accents of chrome, and abstract art. Yet an old paisley shawl with long fringe was draped on a wall above the spinet piano.

Barbara said, 'My mother brought that home from India when she was a college student and had it draped over her grand piano all her life. I'd drape it over the spinet, but Molasses is a fringe freak.'

On Saturday night, before driving to the theater for the musical, the Willows foursome gathered at Barbara's for a light repast.

At the performance, it was the usual happy audience found at *Cats*. The stage was full of furry costumes with tails, and there was a five-piece orchestra in the pit.

Barbara said, 'I should have named Molasses Rum Tum Tugger. He will do as he do do, and there's no doing anything about it.'

Connie cried when Grizabella sang 'Memory'.

At intermission Wetherby said he identified with Bustopher Jones, and Qwilleran said Old Deuteronomy would probably write a newspaper column.

And so it went; Qwilleran was pleased with his new neighbors.

They were all exhilarated as they drove home, until they

heard the disturbing sound of sirens from speeding fire trucks.

Wetherby phoned the radio station, and the voice that came over the speaker shocked them all: 'It's the barn! Your friend's barn, Joe! Arson!'

There was a stunned silence in the vehicle.

Qwilleran was the first one who spoke. 'I'm only thankful that the cats are safe at the condo.'

There were murmurs of agreement from the women. Joe said, 'Do you think there'll be something on TV when we get home? I think we all need a stiff drink.'

Barbara voiced everyone's opinion when she said that the fire was the work of lawless gangs in Bixby. 'They torched the Old Hulk and got away with it because it was of little value, but the barn is known around the world for its architecture and beauty.'

Dr Connie said, 'My friends in Scotland had heard about the barn and asked for snapshots of it.'

Qwilleran said, 'The problem is to distinguish between pranksters and criminals. The new wildlife museum consists of two buildings filled with millions of dollars' worth of mounted animals and art. How do we protect it against these irresponsible marauders? And should we be obliged, in the twenty-first century, to protect our heritage against malicious neighbors?'

173

It was a solemn foursome that arrived at the Willows.

That night the Siamese sensed his feelings; they slept in his bed.

The next morning, Qwilleran walked downtown to the city hall and climbed the back stairs to the police department. Chief Brodie was at his desk, muttering over a stack of papers.

'Well, Andy,' the newsman said, 'it looks as if we've had our last friendly nightcap at the barn!'

'Ach!' was the dour reply.

'Were they the Bixby vandals again?'

'There was more to it than that! We'll talk about it later.' He gave Qwilleran a sour look and waved him away.

Qwilleran walked to the auditorium building and climbed the stairs to Daisy's office.

'Qwill! You'll never believe it!' (Daisy still had her contacts at the Old Manse.) 'A van with a Lockmaster license plate drove away from the Old Manse last night, loaded with Nathan's treasures!'

'That's stealing from a city museum!' Qwilleran said.

Daisy said, 'The good part is that Alma went with them! I hope they catch her.'

* * *

174

Back at the Willows, Koko was waiting with that look of catly disapproval: Where have you been? Was the trip necessary? Did you bring me something?

Koko had known from the beginning that Alma was up to no good. Qwilleran gave the cats a snack and then read to them from the bookshelf. They had finished *The Portrait of a Lady*.

In the days that followed the barn burning, there was no such thing as business as usual in Pickax. The jollity of the coffee shops was reduced to a subdued murmur, and shoppers clustered in twos and threes on street corners, putting their heads together in serious conversation. Even the bankers were more serious than usual.

At the supermarket, customers filled their shopping carts hurriedly and left the store without exchanging chitchat. Qwilleran and his friends felt the same vague uneasiness.

The *Moose County Something* printed editorials, and preachers addressed the subject from the pulpit.

At home, Qwilleran tried to write a trenchant entry for his private journal and was unsuccessful. Strangely, even Koko stalked around on stiff legs, looking nervously over his shoulder.

* * *

Reference was often made to 'The Bad Boys of Bixby'. This nebulous group of ill-doers had for years – probably generations – been blamed for anything that went wrong in Moose County. It was a joke and sounded like a showbiz act. A few years ago, one of them had sneaked across the county line and painted pictures on the Pickax city hall wall, after which he was dumb enough to sign his name.

One day while Kip MacDiarmid, editor in chief of the *Lockmaster Ledger*, was lunching with Qwilleran, he claimed to have found what was wrong with Bixby.

'Moira was trying to sell a marmalade cat to a respectable family in Bixby, when she discovered that indoor cats are prohibited by law in that county. Did you ever hear of such a thing? I think that explains their whole problem.'

'Moose County gave the country trees, gold mines, and fish. Lockmaster gave the country politicians, movie stars, and racehorses. Bixby County gave us a pain in the . . . esophagus!'

Twenty

Following the fire, the arson was the talk of the town, and Qwilleran's phone rang constantly as townsfolk called to commiserate. They meant well, but – in self-defense – Qwilleran stopped answering and let the message service take over.

He welcomed Barbara's call and phoned her back.

She said, 'Qwill, I've been meaning to ask you: could you help me start a private journal like yours? I think it would be rewarding.'

'It would be a pleasure!' he said. 'We can have supper at a new restaurant I've discovered – if you like to live dangerously!'

She accepted, and he made another convert to his favorite hobby. He took two of his filled notebooks as examples – plus a new one to get her started.

After being seated, Qwilleran told Barbara that the restaurant had been started by a member of the Senior Health Club and younger members of her family. It was named the Magic Pebble as a joke, because it was across the highway from the Boulder House Inn.

He said, 'The latter, as you know, is the grotesque pile of boulders as big as bathtubs, which has been famous since Prohibition days.'

Qwilleran handed Barbara a flat stone. 'Do you know what this is?' Without waiting for a reply, he said, 'There's a creek that comes rushing out of the hills into the lake near the Boulder House. The creek bed is filled with pebbles as big as baseballs, but at one point the water swirls them around and flattens them out mysteriously. The natives call them magic pebbles. If you hold one of the flat stones between your palms – and think – you get answers to problems. Even Koko reacts to a magic pebble. He sniffs it, and his nose twitches. Who knows what ideas are forming in his little head?'

During their conference he told her, 'I don't recommend typed pages in a loose-leaf binder. There is something inspiring about the primitive challenge of

178

handwriting in an old-fashioned notebook.'

Barbara said, 'I'm going to dedicate my journal to Molasses on the front page. Whenever I'm sitting in a chair and thinking, he jumps onto the back of the chair and tickles my neck with his whiskers. I sign my entries BH. I have a middle name, but it begins with A and BAH doesn't make a good monogram. When I was in school, the kids called me Bah Humbug.'

Barbara complimented Qwilleran on his Friday column, in which he had urged parents to be more careful in naming their offspring. He often thought parents naming their newborns should consider what the baby's monogram would be. He had gone to school with a nice girl named Catherine Williams, but her parents gave her the middle name of her aunt Olive, and she grew up being kidded about her initials. Also, he knew a Pete Greene whose middle name was Ivan, a fact his friends never let him forget.

Qwilleran liked Barbara's conversation, and they discussed numerous topics.

Barbara asked, 'Are you writing another book, Qwill?'

'Yes, as a matter of fact. On the subject of rhyme and rhythm. I've been writing humorous verse since the age of nine. We had a fourth-grade teacher that no one liked. I wrote a two-line jingle about her that got me in trouble.'

179

He recited: ' "Old Miss Grumpy is flat as a pie. Never had a boyfriend, and we know why." '

'That was precocious for a fourth-grader,' Barbara said.

'I had heard grown-ups talking about her, but I got all the blame. Actually, it solved a problem. The kids went to her class smiling, and Miss Grumpy was less grumpy. Yours truly got reprimanded at school and at home, but I discovered the value of humorous verse. Now I specialize in limericks. There's something about the "aa-bb-a" rhyme scheme and the long and short lines that can only be described as saucy. Its appeal is universal. I know a newspaper editor who carries one around in his pocket. He says he reads it whenever he needs a boost. And cats love limericks. I tested my theory on them. They don't even speak the language, but they respond to the lilt of the rhythm and to the repetition in rhymed words.'

Barbara nodded approval.

Qwilleran said, 'I'm working on the subject of limericks and how humorous verse often solves a problem by making people smile. The guests at the Hotel Brrr were always disgruntled about having to swim in the hotel pool when the temperature was too low in the lake. Now, each arriving guest receives a card with a limerick, and they walk around smiling.

He referred to:

There was a young lady in Brrr
Who always went swimming in fur.
One day on a dare
She swam in the bare,
And that was the end of her.

When they returned to the Willows, Barbara invited Qwilleran in to say good night to Molasses, and he accepted. He liked her range of interests, her forthright advice, her sense of humor. They were met by Molasses, very much in charge of the premises.

'You two have met,' she said as the two males stared at each other. Throwing back his shoulders and taking an authoritative stance, Qwilleran recited:

'Molasses, an elegant cat,
Would not think of catching a rat.
His manners are fine,
He drinks the best wine,
And on Sunday he wears a hat.'

Molasses flopped over on his side, stiffened his four legs, and kicked.

Then Qwilleran broached a subject he was not prone to discuss: Koko's whiskers.

181

'Dr Connie has volunteered to count them when he's sedated for his dental prophylaxis, but somehow I feel guilty because I know he won't approve. He's a very private cat.'

'Then don't do it!' Barbara said. 'What purpose will it serve? Some humans are smarter than others. And some cats are smarter than others!' Qwilleran was impressed by her clearly stated opinion.

'You're right!' he said. 'We won't do it!'